A CURSE A COVEN AND A CANINE

JEANNIE WYCHERLEY

A Curse, a Coven and a Canine:
Spellbound Hound Magic and Mystery Book Two
by

JEANNIE WYCHERLEY

Copyright © 2020 Jeannie Wycherley
Bark at the Moon Books
All rights reserved

Publishers note: This is a work of fiction. All characters, names, places and incidents are either products of the author's imagination or are used fictitiously and for effect or are used with permission. Any other resemblance to actual persons, either living or dead, is entirely coincidental.

No part of this book may be reproduced, distributed or transmitted in any form or by any means, including photocopying, recording, or other electronic or mechanical methods, or by any information storage and retrieval system without the prior written permission of the publisher, except in the case of very brief quotations embodied in critical reviews and certain other non-commercial uses permitted by copyright law.

Sign up for Jeannie's newsletter:
eepurl.com/cN3Q6L
A Curse, a Coven and a Canine was edited by Christine L Baker
Cover design by Graphics by Tammy.

Formatting by Tammy
Proofing by Johnny Bon Bon

*A Curse, a Coven and a Canine
is dedicated with grateful thanks
to Clarissa Place,
a wonderful journalist
full of infectious enthusiasm
and true inspiration for the Clarissa in these pages*

CHAPTER ONE

"Ms Mitchelmore has declined to comment." Clarissa read the words on her screen out loud and wrinkled her nose. After staring hard at them for a moment, she deleted the words Ms Mitchelmore, and instead typed, 'The owner of The Sunshine Valley Pet Sanctuary has declined to comment at this time.'

"Hmm," she sighed, and glanced across at Toby. She'd set up a small desk in the living room, and this provided her with a good view of her spellbound hound, although he was too far away for her to reach out and stroke him. She would have found that comforting.

The medium-sized Schnauzer-cross-whippety-thingie-that defied-both-description-and-definition lay in his bed by the television, his ears relaxed and his mouth open. His black and grey front paws were suspended in mid-air, making little pedalling motions. *Obviously dreaming about squirrels*, thought Clarissa, and turned her attention back to the article on her laptop. It desperately needed completing.

She'd promised to get this copy over to the editor of the *Sun Valley Tribune*, the local newspaper she worked on, by first thing in the morning. Unfortunately, she'd also had a deadline for a piece about vandalism at the local park, as well as a review of a new delicatessen that had opened in town. Filing all three pieces on time meant that tonight at least, she would need to burn the candle a little later than normal.

She took a slug of coffee from her mug and grimaced. Stone cold. The carriage clock on the mantelpiece told her it was ten past two—but it had stopped, and she and Toby had altered the time so that it would always look cheerful. The clock on her laptop display told the stark truth. One-eighteen in the morning.

Clarissa swirled the remaining coffee around her mug and considered making a fresh pot, but if she did that, she'd run the risk of being awake all night needing to pee. She arched her back and then stretched her shoulders. Maybe she'd opt for a swift nightcap instead. Two of her three reports were finished. She could email those across to her boss now, and then have another stab at the kennel fire story first thing in the morning.

She quietly pushed her chair back, not wanting to disturb Toby when he was slumbering so peacefully, but he opened his eyes anyway. Like most dogs, he could have heard a gnat pass wind at a hundred paces. She smiled at him and he closed his eyes again, totally unconcerned. She slipped through to the kitchen and placed her mug in the sink on top of a plate she'd used earlier, before locating a small glass from the cupboard and a tall bottle of sloe gin from the pantry.

She poured an inch of liquid and studied the bottle. Old Joe had distilled the gin himself and left several litres on the bottom shelf of the pantry. She loved the sweet burn on the back of her throat. Her recollections of the old man, her late grandfather, were vague, but all the evidence she'd found around the house led her to believe she would have liked him very much.

Sadly, by the time Clarissa had discovered the existence of her grandfather, Joseph Silverwind had been dead and buried for nearly six months. Toby had been the only witness to his murder, which the police had been keen to write off as a simple stroke. Given the amount of time that had passed by, and factoring in his lowly status as a dog—albeit one that could converse with Clarissa—poor Toby hadn't been able to convince anyone that Old Joe had met his end through suspicious and unlawful means.

Incarcerated in The Sunshine Valley Pet Rescue for six months, and with a death sentence hanging over his head, he'd run away. Clarissa had stumbled across the bereft and lonely dog here in Old Joe's house when she'd come looking for her grandfather. For a while, it had looked like they would lead separate lives, but Old Joe's final will and testament had bequeathed the house, its contents, his meagre savings and, most importantly, Toby to her. She now intended to take care of the dog on her grandfather's behalf for the rest of his life.

In any case, they had permanently bound themselves together, having undertaken a ritual on their first night of legal ownership together, and sworn to track down the woman responsible for his death. They intended to ensure Miranda Dervish paid for the travesty, one way or the other.

Clarissa traced the handwriting on the label of the bottle. Old Joe had traced his letters with a confident flourish. She found herself wondering about him, and who he'd really been. It appeared that he'd lived out the last ten years or so in this house with little contact from the members of his coven, the Coven of the Silver Winds. Was Clarissa to believe he had forsaken magick altogether? She supposed that was a possibility—her parents had done the same after all—but why then had Old Joe been targeted by Miranda Dervish?

Yes, Clarissa and Toby knew exactly who had killed the old man, and they knew she'd stolen a gemstone of some kind from him, but they'd been unable to convince the local constabulary to take action against the perpetrator. Miranda Dervish, or The Pointy Woman as they thought of her, had once claimed to be Clarissa's aunt. She'd turned up at eight-year-old Clarissa's house on the day her parents neglected to come home and escorted her to a school deep in the Somerset countryside. Ravenscroft Lodge had turned out to be a school specialising in magick, sorcery and witchcraft.

Miranda Dervish, it transpired, was no blood relation whatsoever.

Nonetheless, Clarissa had remained at Ravenscroft Lodge until she'd turned eighteen and headed up to the Midlands to study English at University. After that, she'd undertaken a professional apprenticeship on a newspaper in Birmingham before returning to the south-west to work as a junior reporter on the *Sun Valley Tribune*.

An anonymous tip-off that had led her to seek out Old Joe just a few weeks ago had sadly come too late for her to renew her relationship with her grandfather, but Toby had been a true gift. United in their mutual grief, they had pledged to bring The Pointy Woman to justice, somehow, some day.

They hadn't as yet made much headway on that.

Clarissa, leaning against the kitchen cupboard, raised her glass in silent salute. *I haven't forgotten, Old Joe, don't you worry*, she thought, tipping the glass to drain the contents with lip-smacking relish.

Suddenly the ground began to shake beneath her feet, and a deep rumbling sound startled her. All around her the house and its contents vibrated, severely enough that the mug and plate in the kitchen sink clinked together noisily. Clarissa steadied herself, one hand on the worktop. An earthquake of some kind? A fracking tremor?

From the living room came a low growl, fearful yet defensive. The rumble had disturbed Toby too.

A sharp bang on the other side of the wall. Clarissa's head swivelled. It sounded as though something heavy had fallen somewhere in her neighbour's house. Clarissa held her breath, regarding the wall with concern. Mrs Crouch lived on that side, a sweet old lady with a great fondness for Toby.

Clarissa heard the tell-tale pitter-patter of Toby's nails as he ran over the floorboards in the hall. He joined her in the kitchen. "What was that?" he asked.

"I don't know," Clarissa confessed, her voice trembling. "It might have been an earthquake of some kind."

She sounded doubtful, and Toby instantly picked up on this.

"But you think it was something else?" he asked.

Clarissa reached out with tentative fingers and placed her hand on the party wall. With the kitchen units in the way, she couldn't bend over far enough to place her ear against the surface to try and listen, but that would have been assuming she would be able to hear something, anyway. These were solid early twentieth-century houses. The soundproofing here was much better than the student flats or new-builds Clarissa had lived in most of her adult life.

For a moment, she had a clear image of someone on the other side of the wall. A figure in shadow, bending over Mrs Crouch's worktop, mirroring Clarissa's stance. Dark eyes shone with a yellow light.

Unnerved, Clarissa sucked in her breath and jerked away.

The image faded.

"What is it?" Toby asked.

"I don't know." Clarissa's voice sounded hoarse. She looked around. "Can you hear anything unusual?" They stood side by side, straining every one of their senses, Clarissa even holding her breath and hardly daring to blink.

Nothing is ever as oppressive as silence at times such as this, and Clarissa almost jumped out of her skin when a single drop of water dripped from the tap and plinked into the mug in the sink.

She let her breath go, laughing shakily. "It can't have been anything. Just my imagination. We'll see something about a tremor on the news tomorrow."

Toby remained unconvinced, however. "I can't hear anything." Casting a quick glance at Clarissa, he knitted his furry eyebrows together, "but I do *feel* something. Stay here."

He darted through the dog flap, out into the garden. With the light on in the kitchen, Clarissa couldn't see anything through the window. She quickly snapped the light off. The house wasn't completely dark; the lamp from the living room and the backlight of her laptop screen gave off enough for her to see, but also cast the kitchen in shadow. Clarissa moved closer to the sink to peer through the window. She could just about make out Toby, standing ramrod straight on the small square of lawn out there, his shoulders square and his ears pricked, hackles rising. He looked east, towards Mrs Crouch's house, but he wasn't able to see over the fence because of its height and the numerous trees that grew on both sides.

He didn't bark, he didn't whine. He merely listened, his eyes boring a hole into the dark night.

Eventually some of the tension left his body. He walked along the perimeter of the fence sniffing, cocked his leg to water the rockery and sloped back inside through the dog flap.

Clarissa relaxed. "Nothing out there?"

Toby glanced back at the door. "I wouldn't swear to it. But there's nothing to hear. All is quiet in Mrs Crouch's house."

"Any lights on?"

"I couldn't see."

Clarissa considered her options. It might just be a complete over-reaction, but what if it wasn't? "I think I should check out the front."

"I'll come with you." Toby trotted alongside her, so close she could feel his fur on her knee.

"My hero," she smiled.

Under normal circumstances it might have been nice

to take a walk in the open air. The day had been hot and humid, and now the skies were clear and the temperature had reached a balmier 16 or so degrees. If she hadn't been quite so tired, Clarissa might have enjoyed sitting on the step with a glass of sloe gin over ice and gazing at the heavens.

But now, with gritty eyes and nerves that jangled, she trod lightly as she navigated the path to the front gate. She'd yet to replace the old iron gate and it had a tendency to drag on the pavement and creak on its hinges, so she lifted it and swung it inwards as quietly as she could manage.

The rest of Chamberlain Drive remained quiet. A street typical of most early twentieth century English towns, the row of semi-detached houses faced out onto a narrow street face-to-face with an identical row of semi-detached houses. The only differences were in the state of repair, the colour of the front door or the design of the double glazing. For some, the shallow front garden had given way to a parking space and a dropped kerb, but for most, the house was protected by a low stone wall... and that was all the security they had.

Clarissa glanced up and down the street. In a few houses, lights burned in bedroom windows, but for the most part the windows remained shrouded in darkness.

With Toby by her side, Clarissa stepped out onto the pavement and, hugging the wall close, mooched along until she was standing outside Mrs Crouch's property. The gate stood open. That wasn't unusual. The lights in the house were off. That was to be expected.

So far, so ordinary.

But something did give Clarissa pause. The front door appeared to be open. Only a crack. It was not something you would notice unless you were looking.

And Clarissa *was* looking.

Clarissa's insides performed a little shimmy, her heart beat harder and her breath seemed to stick on the top of her chest. Why would Mrs Crouch's door be open at this time of the night unless something was seriously amiss?

Clarissa, treading softly, walked through the gate and up the path. Yes. The door was open, just an inch or so. With the tip of one finger she pushed against the wood so that the door swung a little wider, then tilted her head around it to scour the darkness for any sign of movement. Toby pushed against her knees, demanding access, but she stilled him with her left hand, grabbing his collar and holding onto him. He struggled to go forwards, sniffing frantically.

All of a sudden he shot backwards, almost pulling Clarissa's arm off in his haste to get away.

"Wait!" Clarissa whispered urgently.

"She's been here. She's been here. We need to get out of here."

Clarissa stared down at the young dog. He cowered away from her, or the house at least, the whites of his eyes showing.

"Who's been here?" she asked, confused by his reaction. Did he mean Mrs Crouch?

"We have to get out of here," Toby begged, creeping backwards.

"Toby—"

"The Pointy Woman! The Pointy Woman has been here!" Toby whined, his cries louder now. Clarissa reached for him, trying to calm him down. He would disturb the neighbours, and she didn't dare risk that with him so recently out of the rescue kennels.

"But we need to check on Mrs Crouch," Clarissa told him.

"No point. No point." Toby twisted in her grip and wrenched himself away from her.

"Shhh Toby. It's alright," Clarissa soothed him,

holding out her hand, even though she knew it probably wasn't.

"Nothing is alright." Toby backed away. "I smell death."

And with that he turned tail and ran.

CHAPTER TWO

Clarissa pushed open the door and entered Mrs Crouch's property alone. The house was as still as you might expect at stupid-o-clock in the morning, and yet Clarissa's senses told her something was seriously amiss. Almost as though the very air had been disturbed violently. She remembered the rumble and frowned.

But...

On the other hand, she didn't want to scare an old lady half to death. She tiptoed forwards into the hall. The house exactly mirrored Old Joe's—hers now of course—so she could anticipate the layout. The lights were off everywhere, even upstairs. If there had been any commotion down here, Mrs Crouch had not bothered to come and investigate.

Clarissa poked her head into the living room. The scent of woodsmoke seemed strong, and she found that odd. Embers glowed in the fireplace. Why had Mrs Crouch chosen to light a fire on an evening as warm as this? Clarissa was aware that old people feel the cold more, of course, but even so…

She retreated into the hallway and peered into the kitchen. There were several drawers open here, as though somebody had been looking for something.

Including the cutlery drawer.

Clarissa eyed the long knives in the drawer with some misgivings. Nothing about this felt right. She'd been inside Mrs Crouch's house several times, at the old lady's behest, to share a cup of tea and a chat—you couldn't have called what Mrs Crouch did gossiping. Mrs Crouch, bright-eyed and eager, was an intelligent woman and preferred to discuss literature and current affairs. She never had a bad word to say about anybody.

She was also fastidiously clean and tidy, putting Clarissa to shame.

No. Mrs Crouch would not have left the drawers open when she retired upstairs for the night. Someone else had done this.

Swallowing, Clarissa sloped back to the foot of the stairs. "I smell death," Toby had said. Perhaps now Clarissa should consider simply phoning the police and letting them deal with the situation, but if the old lady needed assistance, the delay in help arriving might make a difference.

"Mrs Crouch?" Clarissa called up the stairs.

No answer.

Clarissa chewed her bottom lip, contemplating what to do next. "Ach," Clarissa cursed. "In for a penny, in for a pound." She started to climb the stairs, gingerly holding on to the railing, in two minds whether to make a noise or not and alert her neighbour to her presence. Halfway up she called again, "Mrs Crouch?"

Still no response.

On the landing, two out of the three doors were closed. Bathroom and back bedroom. Only the front bedroom door stood wide open. The light from the street lamps illuminated the bedroom a little through the curtains, just enough that Clarissa could see that there was nobody in the bed, although given that the covers had been folded back and the pillows disturbed, there must have been recently.

"Mrs Crouch?" Doubt had crept into Clarissa's voice now. She moved forwards more quickly, covering the last few feet of the landing in double time. And there, at the foot of the bed with her nightshirt twisted about her and her eyes closed, lay Mrs Crouch.

Clarissa knelt next to her and felt for a pulse. The

woman seemed cold to the touch and yet, as Clarissa's fingers reached for her neck, the old woman's eyes opened and she reached for Clarissa's hand.

"You're okay," Clarissa promised. "I'm calling for an ambulance now."

The ambulance had taken a while to get to them and in the meantime, a police car had shown up. By then Clarissa had covered Mrs Crouch in her quilt, but in spite of Clarissa's attempt to keep her engaged, the old woman had lapsed into unconsciousness.

Once the paramedics were on the scene, Clarissa took herself down to the front garden in order to be out of everyone's way, and it was here that Toby had re-joined her.

"Honestly," Clarissa muttered. "You're such a prima donna."

"I don't know what you mean," Toby replied, lifting his nose huffily, but avoiding direct eye contact with his human. He didn't know what a prima donna was, but he assumed it wouldn't be complimentary.

Clarissa folded her arms and gave him a scathing look.

"I didn't know she was still alive," Toby sounded

sheepish. "I could definitely smell death." He lifted his nose and scented the air. "But more than that, I can smell *her*."

"You mean—?"

Toby's bright eyes blinked up at Clarissa. "The Pointy Woman."

"You think she's been here?" Clarissa nodded, her face solemn. "I'm inclined to agree. This has her calling card all over it. What did she want?"

"Excuse me, Miss?" One of the uniformed police officers interrupted them. "I just need to take your details and then we won't need to keep you any longer."

Clarissa turned her attention to him. "Of course. I'm Clarissa Page. I—I mean we—" She reached down and stroked Toby's head, "live next door."

"That's number—"

"Thirty-eight. Or *Silverwinds,* as I've called it." Clarissa pointed in the vague direction of the plaque she'd put up on the wall beside the front door, but in the darkness it was impossible to see. Mrs Crouch's house now blazed with light; it seemed the police had illuminated every room and every nook and crevice. The glow emanating from her neighbour's house cast Clarissa's in deep shadow.

The police officer nodded and then motioned for

Clarissa to step aside as the paramedics brought Mrs Crouch out on a stretcher. Clarissa gazed at her neighbour's face, disturbed by how pale the poor woman appeared. "Will she be alright?" Clarissa asked the young policeman.

"It's early days yet. I don't know much more than you, to be honest." The policeman lifted his notebook, ready to ask further questions.

"The door was open," Clarissa told him, repeating her story for the third time. "Do you think someone attacked her?"

"I'm sorry, Miss Page. I can't really discuss that."

Clarissa frowned in exasperation.

"From what I could see, there were no obvious injuries. Perhaps she simply fell out of bed?" the policeman suggested politely.

Clarissa knew that wasn't the case. The position of the bedclothes suggested that the old lady had thrown them back and jumped out of bed, moving around before collapsing or being attacked.

The police officer would not be pressed on further theories, however. He changed the subject. "Do you know if Mrs Crouch has a next of kin?"

"Gosh." Clarissa thought back to their discussions. "I know she was married and her husband passed away quite a long time ago. She's never mentioned children to me."

"Any siblings that you know of?"

"Sorry." Clarissa shrugged and wrapped her arms around herself. The temperature had fallen, and the shock of finding Mrs Crouch on the floor that way had robbed her of her own body heat. She shivered and explained, "I've only been here a few weeks myself, and although we have been friendly and shared pots of tea on occasion, and she feeds Toby far too many treats—"

Toby pricked his ears up, affronted by the notion of 'too many treats'. There could never be such a thing. To his ears, Clarissa had missed out one vital piece of information the police might need in order to pursue their investigations.

"She's a witch you know," Toby told Clarissa.

Clarissa peered down and gave her head a small shake. "No, she isn't," she told the dog.

The police officer raised his eyebrows.

"Yes, she is," Toby argued.

"I think I'd know," Clarissa replied, and turned back to the police officer.

"Well, I think you missed all the clues," Toby replied shortly, and trounced off in the direction of the open front door.

"Er, I don't think you'd better go in there, young man." The second police officer was heading outside and caught Toby by the collar.

Clarissa reached for the dog. "I'm sorry about that. Mrs Crouch loves him. He thinks he has free rein to go where he likes."

"I do," Toby said. "Mrs Crouch said so."

"He's a talkative little fellow, isn't he?" the first police officer asked.

"It's almost like he's trying to hold a conversation," the second police officer laughed.

"Ha ha," Clarissa faked a smile. "Yes."

The second police officer closed the front door and checked it was secure. He held out the keys to Clarissa. "Would you mind holding on to these until tomorrow? Someone will be along to check up on everything and ask you a few more questions, I expect."

"Yes, no problem." Clarissa took the keys.

"And you can phone the hospital in the morning and see how she's getting on. Maybe mid-morning would be best. It will give them a chance to get her settled."

"Will do," Clarissa nodded, and with one hand firmly gripping Toby's collar, she led him back to *Silverwinds*.

Once safely inside the house she let go of Toby,

who fled to his basket, and tossed Mrs Crouch's keys onto her desk. Her laptop had gone to sleep, fed up of waiting for her to resume work. It had now gone three in the morning and her kennel story had yet to be filed.

Clarissa considered her options. She could go to bed, she could finish writing her piece for the paper, or she could try and get to the bottom of Toby's oddness this evening.

Sighing, she threw herself down on the couch.

"Tell me what you know," she said.

It turned out that Toby didn't actually know that much.

"You think she's a witch because she understands what you say?" Clarissa tutted. "She might just be humouring you, darling."

"We have conversations," Toby reiterated. "Just like you and I do. Proper backwards and forwards conversations."

"Not just about treats?" Clarissa checked with him.

"No. I have been telling her stories about my life in the pound and all the dogs I met. She was very sorry that she didn't know what was going on. She says she would have come and rescued me sooner."

Clarissa pursed her lips. This did sound like a dialogue that required some toing and froing between both parties. "Hmmm."

"And you said yourself," Toby climbed onto the sofa next to Clarissa and thrust his head under her hand, "you thought The Pointy Woman had cast a spell that allowed me to speak to all witches. No normal mortal has been able to understand me so far, and you know how hard I've strived to have conversations with everyone."

Again, Clarissa couldn't deny this. No matter where she took him, Toby always had to try and get a word in. For the most part, people dismissed him as an eccentric canine grumbler. Some people loved it. Everyone else ignored him.

Clarissa stroked Toby's head. "But why didn't she tell me?"

"Perhaps she didn't think it mattered."

"Presumably she knew that Old Joe was a witch," Clarissa said.

"I guess so."

"So what's the link between her and Old Joe? Is there one?" It couldn't be a simple coincidence that two witches lived next door to each other in this quiet street.

"The Pointy Woman must think so," Toby reminded her.

Clarissa's hand poised in mid-air. "Are you absolutely sure she'd been in the house?"

Toby sniffed at Clarissa's hands. "Do you know how sensitive a dog's nose is? I bet you've washed your hands a dozen times or more since you woke up this morning, but I can still smell the faint trace of marmalade on your fingers. I know that you bathed in rhubarb bath foam last night and that you've been hanging around with someone who smokes at some stage today."

Clarissa grunted. She'd spent five minutes chatting with one of her colleagues when he'd been taking a cigarette break outside the office.

"I know that you filled up with petrol today and that you had pasta for tea—"

"You know that because you demanded I give you some," Clarissa pointed out.

Toby ignored her interruption. "My point is that scent acts as a record of my life. I memorise smells. I will recognise the scent of The Pointy Woman for the rest of my days."

"You said that she smelled of musty oldness. Is that what you picked up in Mrs Crouch's house?"

"Not just that, but yes, she hasn't changed her perfume." Toby thought back. "There's an undercurrent with her. Something dark and bleak and desperate."

"Dark, bleak and desperate are not fragrances as far as I know," Clarissa retorted, but only mildly. She trusted Toby. She knew he wouldn't be making any of this stuff up.

"She smells of cellars, dark fusty places that rarely see daylight. Old cellars full of antiquated books, dried herbs and the mummified corpses of rodents." Toby cocked his head, trying to think of more examples. "Of places that have no supply of fresh air. There's a scent of the sea about her, but no other sense of anything that is natural. Not even stagnant standing water. Just traffic fumes and the dry huskiness of something deeply sheltered." He'd done his best. He didn't know how to explain it any better than that.

His words disturbed Clarissa and she sat up hurriedly, pushing a hand through her hair. "Perhaps she didn't get what she wanted from Old Joe so she tried it on with Mrs Crouch."

"What about The Six Stone? She definitely took that."

The Six Stone. Clarissa nodded. Her mentor from Ravenswood Hall, Grace Catesby, had identified the gemstone The Pointy Woman had removed from the carriage clock on the mantelpiece as The Six Stone, but what it was and why it was important had so far evaded their understanding.

Clarissa sighed. "She did. Maybe she needed something else? Perhaps she's collecting things?"

Toby yelped. "Like souls?"

Clarissa knitted her brows together in disbelief. "What?" She laughed at the absurdity of it, but not with a great deal of humour. "Souls? Where did you get that idea from? Mrs Crouch isn't dead."

"Yet," Toby muttered.

Clarissa set an early alarm and was up and at her laptop by six. Her lack of sleep resulted in gritty eyes, but coffee helped keep her going and she finally pressed send on her story about the kennel closure just ahead of her deadline at nine. Toby lay as usual, upside down in his basket, eyes closed tight.

She'd started checking her in-box with half a mind on breakfast when Toby suddenly righted himself and jumped out of his basket.

"Morning, snoozy boy," she called, but he ignored her and headed for the hallway.

He sniffed at the crack between the sill and the bottom of the front door. "DC Plum," he announced with confidence, and Clarissa groaned. She'd donned a pair of old shorts and a loose t-shirt when she'd dragged her sorry self out of bed, and hadn't done anything with her hair. The last thing she needed right now was a visitor.

"Just a minute," she called, as she hurriedly yanked a scrunchie from her wrist and tied her hair back. "I'm coming."

She took a quick peek around at the downstairs. It didn't look too bad, although she should really have attended to yesterday's washing up. She shrugged, trotted to the front door and threw it wide open.

"DC Plum," she smiled, as though Toby hadn't already told her and he'd caught her—pleasantly surprised of course—on the hop.

"Ed," he reminded her, although he had his warrant card out and held it up at eye height so she could clearly see it. "How are you doing, Clarissa?"

"I'm fine thanks. A little jaded maybe from a late night." She nodded her head in the direction of the house next door.

"Yes. That's why I'm here." He reached down to

pet Toby. "And what about you, Monster? Staying out of trouble?"

"I'm trying, Ed." Toby wagged his tail. "It's easier said than done though. Clarissa leads me astray."

"Do you mind?" Clarissa growled down at her dog.

Her response only succeeded in confusing Ed. "Who me?" he asked.

"No, sorry. I meant the dog."

"Oh, I'm 'the dog' now, am I?" Toby huffed his way back to the living room.

Clarissa rolled her eyes. "Come on in," she told Ed. "Would you like some tea or coffee? Toast? I haven't had breakfast yet."

"Really?" Ed checked his watch. Quarter past nine. He'd been at work since seven. As far as he was concerned, it was time for a mid-morning snack. Besides, like Toby, hungry seemed to be his middle name. "Tea and toast would be great."

Clarissa nodded and they trooped through to the kitchen where she started multi-tasking. Kettle on the stove, toast in the toaster, hot water running in the sink to start some belated washing up, butter, knives, mugs and plates on the kitchen table, milk out of the fridge. Ed watched her whirl around and marvelled that she could do it all without dropping or breaking anything.

She dished up a cup of dried biscuits in Toby's

bowl and listened for the sound of his feet. He made it into the kitchen in record time. "At last," he told her, starting in on it. "I was fading away!"

"Hardly," she said, not noticing Ed's questioning look.

Once she'd sorted Toby, she turned back to Ed. "Would you like anything on your toast? I'm a big fan of marmalade, but Old Joe had marmite and there's some jam. And cheese, I think." Clarissa opened the fridge and studied the contents. The cheese in its plastic wrapper appeared to have turned blue. And not in a healthy blue cheese kind of way. "Maybe not cheese."

"Marmalade is fine with me, thanks."

Clarissa indicated Ed should take a seat at the kitchen table. He made himself comfortable while she finished preparing breakfast. Sitting opposite him, she poured the tea and pushed a jug of milk his way.

Ed took a bite of his toast while Toby sidled up to him and lay his head on his thigh. "Are you still hungry?" Ed asked.

"Yes," said Toby.

"No," said Clarissa, "he isn't." She prodded Toby. "Behave."

Toby gave Ed his most appealing eyes.

"Ignore him," ordered Clarissa. "He's a total scrounger."

Ed grinned. "That's me told," he winked at Toby.

"She's incredibly bossy," Toby lamented. "I never get a moment's peace. It wasn't like this with Old Joe."

Clarissa fixed Toby with an evil eye. "I'm fairly sure Old Joe didn't feed you human food all the time."

"Not all the time," Toby admitted, but he took the hint and retreated from Ed's thigh. He lay down on the floor with his head under the table, resting it on Ed's foot instead, just to remind the detective of his presence.

"Do you have any idea how Mrs Crouch is?" Clarissa asked Ed.

Ed swallowed hurriedly and washed his mouthful of toast down with tea, reminding himself why he was here. "Not great. The latest I have from the hospital, as of approximately thirty minutes ago, is that she's in a coma."

Clarissa dropped her toast back on her plate in dismay. "Do they have any idea what happened to her?"

Ed shook his head. "Not at this time. They'll be continuing their tests today. It could be a stroke I suppose." He levelled his clear gaze on her, evidently wondering what her thoughts on the matter might be.

"Except—"

"Except?" he prompted.

"The front door was open," Clarissa told him. "I'm sure you know that."

"I'd heard," Ed nodded. "Walk me through what happened last night."

So Clarissa recapped all she'd seen and heard, starting with the rumble and tremor, and finishing with finding Mrs Crouch on the floor upstairs in her bedroom.

"You mentioned the drawers in the kitchen being open." Ed wiped a buttery smudge from his notebook. "What about the living room?" he asked.

"To be honest I didn't turn the lights on in the living room," Clarissa tried to recall her actions. "But I do remember that the fire had been lit sometime yesterday evening."

Ed pulled out his notebook. "The fire was burning? So Mrs Crouch had been up recently?"

Clarissa shook her head. "No, it had died down. But I could smell the scent of woodsmoke."

"And you didn't notice whether anything else had been disturbed?"

"As I said, I couldn't see very well and at that stage, I was only worried about Mrs Crouch."

Toby lifted his head from Ed's foot and interrupted. "Are you going to tell him about The Pointy Woman?"

"Are you sure he's not hungry?" Ed asked.

"No, he wants me to tell you that he thinks The Pointy Woman had been in the house with Mrs Crouch."

"The Pointy Woman? You mean—erm…" He flicked through his notes.

"Sorry, Miranda Dervish."

"Right." Ed pushed his chair back and stared down at Toby. "And he wanted me to know that?"

"Well let's face it, that's why you're here, surely?" Clarissa challenged him. "A murder in this very house not so very long ago, and now a suspicious… suspicious… something next door." Clarissa waved her toast around, almost losing the marmalade as it slid around on a puddle of butter.

Ed wiggled his shoulders in a non-committed way. "I'm just following up the report from last night. I have to confess that your statement about the door being open is of interest to me, but—" Ed waved his notebook at her, "Mrs Crouch is old. She may have forgotten to shut the door herself."

Clarissa pouted. "I don't buy that."

"Neither do I." Toby sat to attention by Clarissa's side and glared at DC Plum.

"She might have forgotten to lock it. We've all done that in the past. But forgotten to shut it altogether? Nah." Clarissa clearly didn't think this was a possibility.

"Well, I have to consider all angles. It may have sprung open by itself."

"I suppose," Clarissa sounded most begrudging. "You'd have to prove that."

"And at the moment," Ed continued, "we don't know whether there was an assault either. As things stand, you know I can't definitely tie in the death of Joseph Silverwind with whatever happened to Mrs Crouch last night. Not without proper evidence."

Clarissa sighed. It sometimes seemed the police couldn't do anything about anything. Their hands were forever tied.

Ed regarded her with sympathy. "You look tired," he said.

"I am."

"Listen. You know Mrs Crouch's house, yes? It would be helpful to me if you could come next door with me now and tell me if you think anything is missing or if anything else besides the kitchen is disturbed? Would you do that? I'll leave you in peace afterwards."

"Of course," Clarissa said. "I mean, I'll help as

much as I can, although I've only been in there four or five times, so I don't know where everything should be or what belongings she had where."

"That's alright." Ed snuck a piece of toast under the table for Toby. "You'll know a lot more than me."

"I don't understand." Clarissa stared down at the fireplace. It had been swept clean.

That wasn't possible.

If there had been a fire in the grate the previous evening, someone had been in this room between three in the morning and now, and thoroughly cleaned it up. Clarissa ran her finger around the grate. It contained no ash, no charcoal, not so much as a smear of soot.

Ed watched her, his face giving nothing away.

"I didn't imagine it." Clarissa rubbed her eyes. Too little sleep. Maybe she was losing the plot. She'd been working hard recently, and with moving into *Silverwinds* and looking after Toby, perhaps things were starting to get on top of her.

"You said you could smell woodsmoke. Might it have come from somewhere else? In the garden perhaps. Or someone else's garden. Perhaps one of your other neighbours had a bonfire or a barbeque earlier in the evening?"

"It's feasible, I suppose," Clarissa replied, "but no. I definitely saw embers in the grate here. It was dying down."

"Hmmm." Ed walked slowly around the room. "Does anything else catch your eye now? Anything unusual?"

Clarissa wandered around after him. She'd sat in here with Mrs Crouch every time she'd visited. Her neighbour had a high-backed three-piece-suite in red velour with embroidered antimacassars, and dark hardwood furniture that comprised a trio of side tables, a bookcase and a sideboard. The furniture appeared old, well-used and perhaps a little dated, but it had been well cared for. A small television sat on a more modern plinth. The window had been hung with both nets and beige curtains with large red roses.

"No. It's as neat and orderly as it always has been when I've visited." Clarissa pulled a face and spun about. "Sorry. I'm not much help."

Ed shrugged. "Don't worry. It's all fine. Remember, it's as much about what's the same as what's different. You're sure nothing appears to have been taken?"

"Not as far as I can see."

They walked through to the kitchen. The drawers

were still open. It looked as though someone had been looking for something and had left in a hurry. Ed peered into each drawer in turn. Clarissa followed his gaze. She could only see the usual kitchen drawer kind of contents. Cutlery in one. Tea towels in another. Odds and sods in a third.

This was the drawer they lingered over. Ed took his pen and carefully moved items around with it. Twine for the garden. A couple of notebooks. Pencils with rubber bands wound around their tops. Packets of wildflower seeds. Batteries. A screwdriver.

"A man drawer," Ed announced. "Nothing unusual here."

Clarissa understood what he meant. The drawer where small things without a proper home languish until a use is found for them. Every home has one. Nothing unusual about it at all.

Apart from the fact that no man had lived with Mrs Crouch for a very long time, Clarissa could only agree. She dutifully followed the detective around the house, peeking inside rooms she'd never had the privilege of entering before. They lingered in the bedroom. Ed examined the state of the bedding from the door. "Can you tell me how the bed looked when you first came in?" he asked.

Clarissa studied the quilt. It had been bundled up,

probably by the paramedics, and placed on the foot of the bed.

"If I remember rightly, the quilt had been thrown back as though Mrs Crouch was getting out of bed. I didn't have the sense that she'd been pulled from the bed."

"There was no disarray?" Ed asked.

"No."

"Intriguing," Ed said. He bent over to take a look under the bed, then hauled out an old suitcase. Popping the clasps, he found another one inside. He lifted it and shook it, then dropped it again and closed the larger suitcase, pushing it back under the bed.

"Rightio. I think that's it for now."

"You don't appear to be treating this as a crime scene." Clarissa couldn't hide her surprise at his slightly cavalier attitude.

Ed frowned. "It's a challenge, a case like this. As with Joseph—your grandfather—what I have here is a case that may simply be nothing more than an old person falling out of bed."

Clarissa shook her head, ready to protest, but Ed held his hands up to placate her. "I promise, I am taking what you say seriously, but at the moment, I don't have any evidence of a break-in or that anything has been stolen. Mrs Crouch's injuries, as far as I know, are consistent with a fall."

Ed gestured at the head of the stairs to indicate Clarissa should descend first. Clarissa resisted the urge to stamp her foot, frowning at the young detective.

"I intend to keep the scene pristine until I know otherwise," Ed continued, "or until Mrs Crouch either wakes up or—" He paused.

He didn't need to complete that thought. Clarissa shivered at the inference. Poor Mrs Crouch.

"Alright," she said, acquiescing reluctantly to his explanation for not being more thorough in his examination of the scene. She knew better though; she was sure of that. She'd just have to find some proof.

Clarissa trotted down the stairs ahead of him, but instead of going straight out the front door she turned back to the living room to have another look at the fire.

It bothered her.

"I really don't get it," she mused aloud. Ed stood at the door watching her. She walked back towards him, glancing around casually and noticing the bookcase to her left. This time something caught her eye. She stopped, intending to take a closer look. Ed stepped into the room, wanting to see what she'd found.

"There." Clarissa pointed out a small scorch mark on the shelf at eye level. As though somebody had left a cigarette burning too long. She reached out to touch it, but Ed stopped her. He pulled out his mobile phone. With a couple of clicks he'd taken a few photos, then he lay his pen alongside the scar on the wood for good measure and took a few more.

"What do you think it is?" he asked. "It looks fresh."

"I have no idea," Clarissa said, but her stomach sank as she followed him out of the house.

Because she'd lied.

She knew exactly what it was.

CHAPTER THREE

Clarissa watched Ed leave, standing on her tiptoes to ensure his car drove down Chamberlain Drive. Even after he had turned left at the top and she could no longer hear his engine, she waited there.

She wanted to make sure he wasn't coming back.

Her mind raced, busy processing what she had seen in Mrs Crouch's house. She badly wanted to go back inside and have another look, without Ed hanging on her coattails, but she feared him returning and catching her in the act of snooping.

How would she explain herself?

She slunk back inside the house, chewing on the inside of her lip and frowning.

"You're going back in there, aren't you?" Toby, perched halfway up the stairs, peered through the banisters at her.

"How did you know?" Clarissa asked. He looked

as though he were behind bars. She'd left him here while she and Ed had ventured next door, mainly because she knew Ed would assume that Toby would contaminate the scene.

"I can just tell." His soft brown eyes regarded her in all seriousness. "Besides. I told you Mrs Crouch is a witch. You didn't believe me, but I think you do now."

"I don't know why you knew that and I didn't."

"Because as I said, she understood exactly what I was saying whenever I spoke to her. We had a long conversation about what my favourite home-cooked treats are, and we decided on cheesy ones. You know cheese is my favourite favourite."

"Well that kind of depends on what hour of the day it is, doesn't it?" Clarissa grinned. "Let alone what day of the week it is."

"She and Old Joe were friends long ago."

"Hmm. Is that right? How can you possibly know that?" Clarissa's voice trailed off. She didn't mean to zone Toby out but she really wanted to get on. She marched through to the kitchen and took a good look around. She couldn't see any of Ed's things, so he'd taken them all away with him. There was no reason for him to come back.

She would risk heading next door again.

Toby pattered down the stairs and followed her

into the kitchen. "She told me. She said they'd first met when they were young people at a festival somewhere. Kind of music and flowers and nature and naked people, I think."

Clarissa screwed her face up. *What was he talking about?* "You've lost me."

She nodded at the front door instead. "Come on, let's go next door."

Toby followed her down the hall but stopped once she'd crossed their threshold.

"What's up?" Clarissa glanced back his way as she made a move to close the door. "Aren't you coming?"

Toby shivered. "How do we know there's no danger?"

"I've just been in there with Ed. If it wasn't safe, I'd know about it, wouldn't I? There's no-one there, I promise. You'll be absolutely fine."

Toby sighed, a deep sigh that he dragged up from the very bottom of his diaphragm. "It's not my safety I'm worried about," he mumbled, and traipsed slowly after Clarissa as she slipped through their gate and along the pavement to the house next door.

The house, calm and quiet without Mrs Crouch's warm personality, reminded Toby in many ways of his own house after the death of Old Joe. He crossed his paws that his cheesy-snack-baking-neighbour would be back to treating duties soon.

Clarissa paused in the hall and watched as he eyed the stairs less than enthusiastically.

"DC Plum had a good look around, didn't he?" Toby asked.

"We can do better. You know that. We have senses that he either doesn't have or he can't utilise as well as we do." She pointed at the living room. "Let's start in here."

Toby mooched through the open door. The first thing he noticed was how incredibly clean the room was. You couldn't describe Mrs Crouch as a sloven by any means—she ran a tight ship where her housekeeping was concerned—but the very absence of the slightest speck of dust or hint of grime was noticeable. He sniffed at the skirting boards and the edges of the rugs and carpets. He peeked behind the curtains and the nets. Not a hint of a dead fly or spider web anywhere. Very little in the way of scent. The room appeared to be almost devoid of any smells at all.

He paused to think, and spotted Clarissa leaning against the door jamb, observing his progress.

"Well?" she asked him.

He cocked his head. "Something's not right. It's like someone came in and gave the place the most thorough clean ever. I mean, it's *so* clean, I can hardly find traces of Mrs Crouch in this room, let alone anyone else."

"Precisely. It's just too sterile in here. Someone used magick to clean this room, maybe the whole house."

She directed his attention to the scar on the wood of the bookcase. "Do you see this?"

He trotted over to take a look. He had to stand on his hind feet and balance his paws against the shelves to see, but he still couldn't. Clarissa picked him up so that he could look at the mark. He snuffled at it, his nose wrinkling as he took in all the information. "I smell wood polish, very faint, and some kind of... burning scent... something charred... and something dark... like old iron."

Clarissa nodded. "Clever boy. This is a wand strike. It's the mark that's left when someone is attacking someone else with hot dark magick. It's intended to hurt, maim, even kill." She stroked the ridged scar, feeling the creases beneath her finger. "I can't swear to it, but I think this is recent."

"Like yesterday kind of recent, I'd say," Toby agreed.

"Follow me into the kitchen," Clarissa said, and he did so, his tail wagging, happy to be of use to her.

Clarissa gestured around the small room, the mirror image of their own. "Have a sniff around here and see what you find."

He dropped his head and methodically swept the room, floorboards and skirting boards first, then lifted his nose to scent the door handles, the cooker, the fridge, the washing machine and kitchen units. He sniffed thoroughly under the table, then finally returned to the area he found most interesting.

The 'man drawer', as DC Plum had called it. Ed had closed the drawer after he'd sorted through it, but it had been open when Clarissa had first investigated the mysterious noise the night before.

Toby sank back onto his haunches. "She was definitely here," he announced to Clarissa. "The Pointy Woman."

"You can smell her?" Clarissa wanted to make sure.

"Only just. It's incredibly faint." That fustiness. The stagnant air. Something long buried. Toby shuddered. Unmistakably her.

Clarissa expelled her breath noisily and pulled open the drawer again to scrutinise the contents. "What would she have been looking for in this drawer, I wonder?" She opened the drawer next to it and plucked out a fork, using that to move items around as she'd seen Ed do with his pen. There were rubber bands and fuses, a couple of old beer mats, the instruction guide for a toaster, and the plastic cap you might use to cover an open can of baked beans.

Nothing jumped out at Clarissa.

She shook her head, exasperated by the lack of clues. "Whatever it was, she must have found it."

Toby jumped up and peered down into the drawer too, eyeing the contents with interest. Clarissa could have reprimanded him for counter-surfing; she needed the house to stay as pristine as possible, after all. If Mrs Crouch didn't make it, then DC Plum would have to open an investigation into her death. The last thing she wanted was to have to explain exactly why Toby's pawprints or hair were littering the previously immaculately-preserved scene.

But Toby leaned forwards, his paws scrabbling to allow better access, his nose reaching to the furthest part of the drawer.

"What are you doing?" Clarissa asked, grabbing hold of his collar in an attempt to restrain him. "You're going to damage the drawer if you're not careful."

"I see something!"

"Where? Get down. Let me have a look."

Toby reluctantly dropped down. "You have to get down to my level."

Clarissa bent at the waist and peered into the drawer.

"No. You're still too high. Get lower down."

Clarissa grunted in exasperation but dropped to her knees until her eyes were at the same height as his, as he suggested. At first, she didn't think it made a difference. Down here she could hardly see the contents of the drawer unless she stretched up and peered over the edge of the wood. "I still don't see anything," she complained.

"That's because you're looking into the drawer, try looking behind it," Toby explained with maddening and exaggerated patience.

Clarissa tutted in annoyance. "I'm not wearing X-ray specs—" But then she spotted what he meant. A glow, virtually imperceptible, but there nonetheless. Like someone had switched on a light behind the drawer unit. It lit up the white of the inner wood of the cabinet, casting a slight tinge of blue.

"Whoa. What is *that*?" Clarissa, still on her knees, yanked at the drawer. It came out a long way, but something, either a mechanical construction or a magickal one, held the drawer firmly in place. She yanked harder, but it didn't give an inch.

"Weird." Clarissa frowned. "This is a fairly cheap

kitchen. You would imagine I could destroy it quite easily."

She scuttled backwards and opened the cupboard door beneath the drawer. Pots and pans were kept in here, and now she hauled them out. They clanged together loudly as she piled them to one side—and Toby backed off, not appreciating the din at all—until the cupboard stood empty.

"There's nothing here!" Clarissa grumbled.

Toby nudged her elbow, squeezing his head between her and the wall of the cabinet. "Let me see."

She edged sideways and allowed him access, his claws sliding on the slippery base of the cupboard, built from little more than cheap MDF. "It's coming from up here. Behind the drawer," he called back to her, his voice reverberating in the confined area. He struggled to reverse out, so Clarissa helped by guiding his rump. "You'll need to get your fingers up there behind the drawer," he told her.

Clarissa nodded and edged her shoulders into the space he'd vacated. There wasn't a huge amount of room for her, and the struts of the cabinet made it difficult. "I could do with a torch," she mumbled.

"There's one in the man drawer," Toby replied helpfully.

Clarissa withdrew from the cabinet, banging her head on the drawer as she tried to stand up. "Ow!"

"Sorry about that." Toby wagged his tail in sympathy, as Clarissa dug through the contents of the man drawer, much less carefully than before, locating a torch and a screwdriver. The small black torch would have easily fitted inside a woman's handbag. Clarissa pressed the button on the end and a powerful light came on.

"Once more with feeling," she said and dived back into the cupboard.

She scooted in as far as she could, and dug her elbows close to her torso, simply using her wrists to manoeuvre her hands into a better position to shine the torch. At first, she couldn't see anything. The glow emanated from somewhere above her head but, because of her size in the limited space available, she couldn't get her head to twist far enough to peer up through the gap behind the drawer's runners.

She squeezed herself more tightly into a ball and pressed her left cheek hard against the back wall of the cupboard. Now, by squinting upwards, the torch aimed through the slender gap, she spotted a lump against the back of the drawer, less than the size of a small matchbox. She swapped the torch into her left hand, switching it with the screwdriver, and then eased her elbow up as high as she could, inching with her fingers, extending the screwdriver until it made contact with the softly glowing lump.

She wiggled the screwdriver back and forwards, shining the torch up so that she could see what she was doing, until the lump suddenly shifted and bright blue light spilled out, threatening to blind her. She snapped her head back, her crown colliding with the back wall of the cupboard.

"By all that's green!"

"Are you alright in there?" Toby pushed himself in, making a tight squeeze even worse.

"Out! Out!" Clarissa pushed him away and dropped the torch, then shifted herself back against the wall, blinking up at the light. "I almost had it then."

"One more push," Toby said. "I've got all my paws crossed you do it this time." He licked Clarissa's face.

"Will you get out of it? I can't do it with you this close."

Toby placed one paw in the centre of Clarissa's stomach, causing her to jump and bang her head again. "*Toby!*"

"I'm only trying to help."

"No. You're just very trying." Clarissa clenched her teeth. "Get. Out."

"Okay, okay." Toby reversed out, and Clarissa

squinted back up at the lump. Once her eyes had adjusted to the warm blue light, shining out so incredibly brightly, she could discern the shape more clearly. It actually appeared to be a wad of duct tape or something similar.

Somebody, perhaps Mrs Crouch, had taped an object to the rear of the drawer.

Clarissa slipped the screwdriver up into the gap and wiggled and wriggled it around until finally, the duct tape came free and the lump fell onto the wood above her head. Clarissa hooked her hand into the gap and managed to get a tenuous grasp of the tape with the very tips of her fingers and drag it loose. It plopped onto her chest, surprisingly heavy.

"Have you got it? What is it?" Toby barked excitedly, nearly deafening her.

"Ssshh!" Clarissa slid out of the cupboard, moaning with relief that she could stretch out at last. She plucked the wad of tape from where it had landed and sat cross-legged on the floor. Toby sidled up close to her, insinuating his head between her arm and her chest.

"What ya' got? What ya' got?"

"Cover your eyes," Clarissa instructed him, and fiddled with the tape, using her nails to rip it loose, piece by piece, until suddenly the kitchen was bathed in a beautiful sky-blue light that rippled against the walls and cabinet doors.

"Wow!" Toby blinked, following shards of light as they danced around the room.

"Toby?" Clarissa drew his attention back to what lay on the palm of her hand.

He snuffled at it. "It looks like a coloured stone."

"A gemstone. Like The Six Stone? Do you remember?"

"The one The Pointy Woman took out of the carriage clock?"

"Yes, except that one was purple." Clarissa held the stone at eye height, clasping it gently between thumb and index finger. It shimmied in the light.

"It's so beautiful," Toby whispered. "I can see why The Pointy Woman would want it. It's treasure."

"That's true," Clarissa said. "Except *she* doesn't strike me as the sort of person who would want something simply because it looked beautiful. I'll bet there's an entirely different motive for stealing these stones."

"Maybe they have some magickal powers?" Toby regarded the stone with interest. It looked innocuous enough to him. It hadn't turned him into a pillar of salt or burned a hole in Clarissa's clothing or the palm of her hand.

And yet...

"You could be right." Clarissa scrutinised the stone, flipping it gently over so she could view it from a different angle. It had flattened sides but was an otherwise perfect circle. "The Six Stone as far as we know was star-shaped, wasn't it?" The hollowed area they had found in Old Joe's carriage clock had been star-shaped. "What if these stones are from a group of stones?"

"And each one is a different shape, you mean?" Toby asked.

Clarissa nodded. "Maybe they're not even connected to each other. Perhaps they're just pretty gemstones."

"But why does The Pointy Woman want to collect them all?" Toby asked.

His eyes met Clarissa's. The Pointy Woman had killed Old Joe and they suspected she was behind the attack on Mrs Crouch.

"She wants these stones pretty badly," Clarissa frowned.

Toby swallowed. "And it seems she'll stop at nothing to add to her collection."

CHAPTER FOUR

"She didn't get what she wanted." Toby experienced a shiver that ran from the top of his scalp to the tip of his tail. He shook himself out. "Not this time."

Clarissa created a fist around the stone. Blue light bled from between her clamped fingers. She looked around for some kind of container to put it in for safekeeping and spied a small canister near the bread bin. When she popped the lid off, the unmistakeable scent of cheese wafted through the air. Mrs Crouch's homemade dog treats. She dropped the stone inside and rammed the lid on quickly before Toby could demand a snack, but as she looked over at him, feeling a little guilty—because after all, he'd been the one to find the stone—she realised he seemed a little downcast.

"What's wrong, mate?"

"You know she'll come back, don't you?" he asked, his voice small and plaintive. "The Pointy Woman."

This had occurred to Clarissa. "We'll need to be prepared." She tried to sound more confident than she felt. "And we'll have to find a safe hiding place for the stone while we investigate what it is, what it does and where it belongs."

Toby, his head and tail down, still looked worried. "The Pointy Woman knew vaguely where to find it. She'd been investigating this drawer."

He had a good point. "Yes, she had. But she must have been interrupted."

"When you came into the house, maybe?" Toby suggested.

Clarissa considered this. It was possible but unlikely. A little time had elapsed between hearing the noise from next door and feeling the building vibrate and her and Toby turning up on the doorstep. "I didn't have a sense that there was anyone still in the house when we arrived here last night, did you?"

Toby had to admit he hadn't, but he'd been in such a panic about The Pointy Woman that he feared he might have misread the signs. He didn't want to admit that though, so he remained silent.

Clarissa clamped her hand on top of the treat tin. "Before we head home, I want you to take a quick look in the bedroom with me."

Toby obediently followed her up the stairs,

glancing at the closed front door with something amounting to trepidation as he passed it. The Pointy Woman was out there somewhere. Maybe she was watching them. He knew she wouldn't give up easily. What was to stop her coming after him again? Or even worse, what if she targeted Clarissa?

He'd lost one person he loved; he couldn't let that happen again.

Clarissa ushered him into Mrs Crouch's bedroom. "Have a look around," she told him, and he set to once more, snuffling and sniffing and investigating all corners and hidey holes. This room, while clean, had experienced far less magickal interference than the living room downstairs. He could pinpoint the area where Mrs Crouch had been found. He scented that spot for a while, but it didn't tell him much.

Finally, he dropped onto his belly and slid along the rug under the bed.

"I don't think there's much under there." Clarissa had checked earlier while Ed had been with her. The detective had pulled a few items out, but as he'd said, given this wasn't yet a murder case, it had been a cursory glance at best.

"Just a bag of old clothes and a suitcase," Toby called out. "Did you check inside it?"

"Yes. It had another—smaller—suitcase inside."

Clarissa's upside-down head appeared at the edge of the bed.

"I'd have another look if I were you," Toby said. "It smells interesting to me."

"Does it smell like The Pointy Woman?" Clarissa asked, hauling the suitcase from under the bed. Toby followed it out, shaking himself to get rid of the dust devils he'd managed to coat himself in.

Clarissa popped the clasp of the large suitcase. This was an old-fashioned affair, covered in battered once-cream leather, now badly scuffed and marked. The little clasps were gold. Clarissa couldn't imagine for a moment this ancient relic would last very long in the hold of a modern aeroplane.

It contained, as she'd witnessed when DC Plum had originally pulled it out, another smaller leather suitcase, this one in dark green. As well as the clasps, this one had large buckles. Ed had shaken the case, but not bothered to open it. Now Clarissa lifted it free and found, as he had, that it didn't have a great deal of weight to it. She placed it on the floor and unthreaded the leather straps, popped the clasps and opened the case. Inside she found a large manila file; the very colour and thickness of the cardboard seemed to date it. Several large elastic bands had been wound around it at some stage. But these had perished, and as

Clarissa opened the cover, they fell to the floor like desiccated worms.

Toby peered over her shoulder, sniffing along with interest as Clarissa picked through the contents. Old newspaper clippings - dozens and dozens of them, photos - the colours faded in many cases, numerous letters, and a small notebook covered in midnight blue leather, tied with a leather thong.

"What are we doing?" Clarissa flipped the cover of the manila folder over, attempting to cover everything up. She quickly realised that now the contents had been disturbed, it was kind of like stuffing eels into a small bucket; things were slipping out everywhere. "We probably shouldn't be looking at this stuff. It's Mrs Crouch's personal property. Nothing to do with us."

Toby placed a paw on a photo that had slipped to the floor despite Clarissa's fumbled attempts to shuffle everything back into place. "Is this not Old Joe, though?"

"How can you see that?" Clarissa asked, reaching for the photo. "I didn't think dogs had such good vision."

"Hey. There's nothing wrong with my eyesight, okay?" Toby tried to take the photo from her but she held it aloft so they could both look at it. A man with dark brown hair and impressive sideburns, probably in his mid-to-late thirties and a woman, younger, her hair long, a smattering of freckles across her face. They were both smiling—but at each other, not the photographer.

"You think this is Old Joe?"

"In his younger days." Toby pawed at Clarissa, wanting the photo for himself, but she pushed him away.

"So who's the woman?" Clarissa flipped the photo. On the reverse the words, '*Solstice Fayre 1974, JP and me*'.

"It looks like Mrs Crouch to me."

"How can you tell that?" Clarissa dropped her hand to study Toby's face. "Since when has a dog ever been able to look at a photo and pick out the people in it?"

Toby cocked his head, blinking rapidly. "I don't know. Maybe I've never actually tried to do it before, but I always could?"

"Ha. That's pretty unusual, I'd say." Clarissa showed him the photo again. "Could you do this before The Pointy Woman cast a spell on you?"

Toby took a moment to think back. Prior to the moment Miranda Dervish had walked into Old Joe's house, he'd thought he'd been living an ordinary dog's life. Playing in the park with his neighbourhood friends, moonlit late-night walks on the lead under the street lights, breakfast and an evening meal lovingly prepared by Old Joe, and afternoon snoozes on the sofa. It had been wonderful.

But everything had changed when Old Joe's killer had pointed her claw-like fingernails at him. He understood that before, he'd lived his life at one step removed, akin to living in a bubble surrounded by soft cushions. Now everything seemed clearer, louder, somehow more in focus. His senses were razor-sharp in a way he'd never previously experienced.

"Maybe not," he admitted.

Clarissa studied the photo herself once more. "You know, I think you're right. This does look very much like a young Mrs Crouch." She opened the folder and placed the photograph on the top. "It proves what you were suggesting, that Mrs Crouch and Old Joe had a history together."

"Surely that means that the folder is partly ours?" Toby enquired, his tail wagging almost politely. "After all, we represent Old Joe's best interests."

"I'm not sure it works that way," Clarissa smiled. She returned the folder to its suitcase within a suitcase. "It's really none of our business."

She stood up. "Come on, let's phone the hospital

and see how Mrs Crouch is doing. Maybe she's awake and we can ask her in person."

Toby followed Clarissa slowly out of the bedroom, glancing back at the suitcase now stowed safely under the bed, reluctant to leave it there where anybody could find it if they looked hard enough.

"Toby, let's go," Clarissa called to him. "I want to store this gemstone safely at home. You need to help me find somewhere."

It doesn't matter where you hide something, if someone wants what you have badly enough, they'll find it, he thought. But he trotted obediently after Clarissa.

He liked to be a good boy.

Chapter Five

"You have some mail." Toby trotted in from the living room where he'd been snatching a post-breakfast nap in his freshly laundered soft and squidgy basket. Every morning he woke up in his comfortable bed, was a morning he could treasure. Now he performed a couple of luxurious stretches; first a downward dog, then a reverse downward dog with added back foot stretch and nose point. He ended by sitting bolt upright and stretching his neck and head as high as he could. Clarissa heard the click of bones and shuddered.

"Couldn't you have brought it in for me?" she asked. She'd slept like the dead the previous night after the disruption of the night before, and although she was due to check in at the office sometime this morning, she was still eating breakfast in her pyjamas, while sitting at her desk and answering work emails.

She called it multi-tasking. She'd fully intended to complete another story for the paper, but truthfully, she'd lost track and drifted away, pondering on Mrs Crouch and what her link to Old Joe and The Pointy Woman might be.

She took a bite of toast. It had already gone cold.

"Me bring the mail?" Toby protested. "I'm not a retriever."

Clarissa snorted. "You haven't a clue what you are, Mr Liquorice Allsorts. There may well be retriever in there somewhere."

"I could take offence at that," Toby replied with a disdainful sniff, "but I won't. As long as you give me your crust corners."

Clarissa regarded her remaining breakfast. "I'll give you *a* corner if you go and get the post."

Toby considered her counteroffer. "One corner? That's a bit mean."

"You, my son, are putting on weight." Clarissa pointed at his mid-riff. "And the vet won't tell *you* off for your manipulative ways and appealing eyes, will she? No. It'll be me that gets an ear-bashing."

Toby's bushy eyebrows knitted together in a frown. "I'm insulted by that. I need to put some weight on. I had a traumatic six months. I was underfed."

Clarissa decided to let this go. Toby had indeed

suffered a traumatic six months after being sole witness to the murder of Old Joe. His incarceration in the local rescue pound hadn't been easy on him and he'd come very close to being put to sleep.

"One corner. Final offer. Mmm, yummy!" Clarissa waved a corner of her toast at Toby. "So, what about it, furry boy?"

Toby huffed. "Alright." He trotted down the hall, his claws making their usual pitter-patter noises on the wooden floor. There were three envelopes, bound together with an elastic band, which made it easier for him to pick up. He brought them back to Clarissa, his tail wagging at the prospect of toast.

Clarissa took the bundle from him. The elastic band reminded her of the folder hidden in the suitcase under Mrs Crouch's bed. The hospital hadn't shared much the previous day when Clarissa had phoned them. The elderly neighbour's condition was described as 'stable'.

Whatever that meant.

"Probably bills," Clarissa grumbled, and flicked through them. One was addressed to Old Joe. She'd notified as many people as possible about his passing, but never a day went by without something new appearing in the post. It seemed Old Joe had been a voracious letter writer. Clarissa put this envelope to one side to deal with later. The second was a flyer from a local garden centre offering great deals on patio furniture and barbeques, while the third, a plain white envelope with a window, had been addressed to her.

She tore it open and pulled out the single typewritten sheet inside.

Toby nudged her with his nose. "A deal's a deal."

She absently handed over the agreed corner of butter-congealed toast and Toby chomped it down. He looked up at her expectantly, ready to demand her other corners, but Clarissa's face had fallen.

"Are you alright?" Toby asked in alarm. "Is it bad news from the lawyer?"

Toby lived in fear that Old Joe's lawyers wouldn't fully hand over the house to Clarissa—part of her inheritance—which would essentially leave the pair of them homeless. The lawyers had been slow in dealing with Old Joe's probate up to now, but Clarissa remained cautiously optimistic that everything would turn out alright in the end.

"No, it's from the CEO of Photia Group Newspapers. That's the company that owns the *Sun Valley Tribune*." Clarissa placed the piece of paper down on the table in front of her and smoothed it out, her toast completely forgotten. She rubbed her forehead with her right hand and Toby noticed it tremble a little. He whined in concern and placed his head on her thigh.

"What is it?" he asked.

Clarissa's voice wobbled. "I've been fired."

Toby started back in alarm. What did 'fired' mean? He studied Clarissa in open-mouthed consternation, before hastily sniffing her clothes. She didn't smell of smoke. Perhaps she was mistaken. "Fired?"

"They don't want me to come to work anymore. I don't understand." Her eyes shone with hot tears. "I've been there eighteen months and I spoke to my editor just the other day. He told me my work has been exemplary. I just don't get it." She swallowed. She'd always enjoyed her job, although she hoped to eventually work her way up to be taken more seriously as an investigative journalist. The *Sun Valley Tribune* had been the first rung of a tall ladder, but still... to lose her position this way, so early in her career. How was that going to look?

"Fired? Can they just... do that?" Toby looked up at his friend. He found the notion of employment and unemployment slightly perplexing. Old Joe hadn't worked, because Old Joe had been old. Toby had come to expect everyone to take naps whenever they felt like it, to eat whenever they were hungry, to walk in the park when the weather was fine, or to watch old films when it rained. This had been the cycle of his days.

However, living with Clarissa as his primary human had been a bit of an eye-opener. She went out to work nearly every day. He would sniff her clothes when she came down from her bedroom and he would know what she intended to do. Work clothes were very different to leisure clothes. They were smarter, although functional. Going-out-for-a-walk clothes and slobbing-around-the-house clothes were his personal favourites.

He'd adapted though. Clarissa worked fairly flexibly and sometimes came home for lunch or even took him out with her. Occasionally she had to go somewhere in the evening to watch a performance at the theatre or cinema or a school, and he'd be left alone, but then she'd spend time with him the following morning. Most Saturdays she attended sports events or fetes, along with a photographer, for at least a few hours, but then the rest of the weekend was theirs to do with as they wished.

Now all that seemed to hang in the balance.

"Apparently they can." Clarissa re-read the letter. Huge tears ran down her nose and dropped onto Toby's head. He hurriedly stood and tried to climb onto her lap to give her a good facewash. "Don't be sad,

Clarissa," he begged. "What can I do to make it better?"

"I'm not sure there's anything anyone can do," Clarissa croaked, her voice hoarse and her nose running. "Darn it. Just when I thought I could settle down a little bit."

This distressed Toby even more. Couldn't they settle down now? Would she leave him? Would he have to go back into the kennels? He wailed, and Clarissa wrapped her hands around his head to shush him.

"Why can't we settle down?" he mumbled as she scruggled his ears.

Clarissa blinked back her tears. "I didn't mean 'we' can't. I'd kind of hoped I'd found a way to keep us in biscuits for the foreseeable future. I need to have an income, is all I meant. I thought this position with the *Sun Valley Tribune* would see me through for a few years."

She released him and offered up her now-cold toast. Toby accepted it and chewed on it more thoughtfully than he had the last piece. "So," he asked once he'd swallowed, "why have they fired you?"

Clarissa puffed out her cheeks. "They are claiming that I brought the newspaper into disrepute by reporting on the instance where the Sunshine Valley

Pet Sanctuary handed over Miss Phoebe to a couple pretending to be her owners."

"But that was the truth!" Toby scowled. "You rescued her and highlighted the kennel's lack of care."

"Which was completely inexcusable," Clarissa agreed. "Even so, I was careful not to name names, but I think the subsequent fire at the kennels and the furore surrounding the police investigation kind of gave the game away. Everyone knows who I was referring to."

Toby looked alarmed. "Do you think someone has complained about you?"

Clarissa shook her head, quick to dismiss the suggestion, but his words struck home. She stared at her dog in stunned silence for a second, before whispering, "Sue Mitchelmore, you mean?"

"Perhaps. But I wouldn't put it past The Pointy Woman either, would you?" Toby asked.

Clarissa clapped a hand to her mouth. "She's more than capable of being that vindictive, isn't she? Oh my word. What's that saying? Just because you're paranoid, it doesn't mean they're not out to get you."

Toby burrowed his head into Clarissa's lap. She exhaled noisily. "I have to go in and collect my things and have a word with the manager. Maybe I'll ask him about whether they've received a complaint from someone. And who knows? Perhaps they'll rethink their decision." She didn't sound hopeful.

"I could come with you," Toby offered.

"I'd like that," Clarissa smiled.

"I'm sorry, Clarissa." Jarvis Winslow readjusted his spectacles and peered down at the letter she'd given him. The one she'd received from Photia Group Newspapers a little less than an hour ago. "I've heard from the boss too, on my email this morning."

"Have they given any kind of explanation?" Clarissa fought to keep a lid on the tears that threatened to spring unbidden to her eyes once more. Jarvis inhabited an office rather like a goldfish bowl. It had glass on three sides and a great view of the general work area, where three of Clarissa's colleagues were engaged in writing, researching, proofing and creating a print layout for this week's Friday edition.

Jarvis pulled the corners of his mouth down. A nerdy-looking skinny man of around forty years of age, he'd always been supportive of Clarissa's career at the *Sun Valley Tribune*. "They pretty much replicated this letter." He returned her copy. "You can have a look at mine if you like? See for yourself?"

Clarissa bit down on the side of her cheek, absolutely determined not to start crying, and bent down to make a fuss of Toby, effectively hiding her face from her boss. "No, it's fine," she said. If his missive wouldn't tell her anything she didn't already know, what was the point?

Jarvis hesitated. "You know, I'll be honest with you. I'm shocked. I've never known anything quite like it. I've been the editor here for eight years and I've never been told to let a member of staff go in this fashion. It's all very odd."

"It's because of the kennels story we ran," Clarissa said, and fondled Toby's ears.

"Yes. But there was nothing wrong with that story. I thought you handled it well. A public information piece. No names mentioned. As far as I was concerned, I didn't have any problem with running it." He threw himself down into the chair behind his desk. "No-one has tried to rap my knuckles about it, so I'm not sure why they're gunning for you."

Toby pulled free of Clarissa's grasp and walked around the desk to confront Jarvis. "It's because of The Pointy Woman," he told the editor. "You ought to be investigating her."

Jarvis drew away and regarded Toby with wary suspicion. "He's not going to attack me, is he?"

"No, of course not." Clarissa smiled in spite of her misery. She walked around the desk to retrieve Toby and clipped his lead on. "He thinks there's an ulterior motive. Someone out to get us."

"Us?"

"Me, I mean."

"Who might that be?" Jarvis had been desk-bound a long time but he'd started as a street reporter, and now his curiosity had been piqued.

"Oh, don't worry. I'm sure it's nothing." Clarissa didn't fancy explaining herself to Jarvis. He'd always been decent to her, but this whole debacle would be way out of his realm of understanding.

Jarvis shifted in his seat. "If you think a third party has a hand in all this, maybe we could talk to human resources?"

Clarissa blew out her cheeks. It seemed like a lot of trouble. The *Sun Valley Tribune* was a small enterprise, part of a group of papers around the United Kingdom. Human resources were based in Manchester where Photia Group Newspapers had its head office, and where the CEO lauded over the workforce.

"All this has to have come from them in the first place," Clarissa shrugged. "If anything could be done, I'm sure they would have."

She edged backwards towards the door. "I'd better clear my desk. If you could see your way to writing a good reference for me when the time comes?"

"Ah." Jarvis shifted in his seat. "Therein lies a small problem."

"What problem?" The tremble in Clarissa's voice was unmistakeable. Toby pressed himself against her knees.

"I was advised that I couldn't write you a reference. Not on our headed notepaper. I... erm... you... you'll have to approach HR, and they will provide a generic reference on PGN headed paper."

"Generic?" Clarissa hadn't meant to shriek, but through the glass, she spotted several of her now ex-colleagues glance up from their screens, curious about the scene unfolding in Jarvis's office.

Grimacing, Jarvis loosened his tie. "I know. As I say, it's all untoward. I've never known such a situation. Nothing so severe as this over one fairly straightforward and innocuous story."

Clarissa dashed a hand at her eyes. Fear and despair combined to create a lump in her throat. She reached down to ruffle the fur on Toby's head. "I think you're right," she told the dog. "We've made an enemy."

They sat together on a park bench. Clarissa had unclipped Toby's lead and had expected him to run joyfully around, sniffing the heady scents of summer and other dogs' pee-mails but instead, he'd climbed up onto the bench next to her and laid his head in her lap while she snuffled into a paper handkerchief.

"It wasn't much of a job, just a place to start my career, but I enjoyed it," she sniffed eventually.

Toby lifted his head. It appeared her tears hadn't completely dried up and, judging by the shininess of her eyes, there were plenty more to come.

"You'll find another position on another paper," Toby made an attempt to console her. "You're a brilliant reporter." He had no idea whether this was true or not, but it sounded like the right thing to say. He could imagine Old Joe saying such a thing.

"But where?" Clarissa sniffed. "There aren't that many newspapers down here. Most of them are in the big towns and cities."

Toby considered this information with a certain amount of alarm. He didn't want Clarissa to move. Not under any circumstances. He wanted to remain in Old Joe's house forever. And he wanted Clarissa to stay with him. "No witchy newspapers?" he enquired.

"Or magazines that witches read? *Auto Broomstick? Witches Weekly? House and Familiar?*"

Clarissa twisted her head slightly to smile at him. "Where have you heard of those?"

Toby shrugged. "I thought I was making them up."

Clarissa laughed and her pale face lit up. It gave Toby joy to witness it. "You probably are. But even those would be based somewhere fairly central. Not down here in the land that time and modernity forgot."

"Just write stuff and send it to them." Toby sat up straight so that he and Clarissa were almost at similar eye-level. "I would imagine that the thing about writing for publications run by witches, is that they're less likely to be intimidated by one of their own. They'll know the tricks. They'll know the difference between good witches and bad witches, and either they'll care, or they won't, but at least they'll be transparent about it all."

Clarissa opened and closed her mouth like a goldfish. *How could Toby know all this?*

Toby had started to warm to his theme. "You want to be an investigative journalist, right? Well, that means digging around and—well—investigating things. Not turning up to junior football sessions on a soggy Saturday in September, or interviewing flower arrangers at the Church fete, or pandering to the promotional demands of self-published writers." Toby wiggled his ears. "You know what you need to do, Clarissa?"

"What?"

"Write an investigative story about The Pointy Woman and the murder of Old Joe and send it to the biggest witchy newspaper there is. Make them pay you for it, and then buy me lots of treats and tuna sammiches!"

"Tuna?" Clarissa narrowed her eyes.

"That's my favourite favourite."

"Today at least." Clarissa reached out and smoothed the spiky fur on top of Toby's head, considering his suggestion. Perhaps the time was ripe for her to progress her career goals. She'd always imagined she would work in-house with newspapers, but maybe today's unexpected events would lead her down a different path. Why shouldn't she freelance? If she was half as good as people had told her, then she would have nothing to fear.

Yes, she'd be without an income for a while, but she had some savings as well as the small nest-egg that Old Joe had left her, and of course, because he'd bequeathed her the house, she didn't need to pay rent.

She and Toby would have to be frugal for a while until she managed to start earning a decent income.

But not today. There could be a little leeway in the budget for lunch.

"You may well get your tuna sammich, Toby. I think you might be a secret genius."

"Oh, make no bones about it," Toby jumped off the bench and danced in front of her. "There is no secret about my genius."

Late that evening, with jazz playing softly in the background and Toby snoozing contentedly in his basket, Clarissa opened up her laptop and began to work. For a few hours she made notes of potential publications, their contact details and the kind of stories they liked to publish. From there, she began to jot down a few potential story ideas she could work on over the next few days. She intended to draft a few proposals and pitch them to editors to gauge interest in her work.

As the news came on the radio at midnight, Clarissa rubbed her tired eyes and yawned. Time enough tomorrow to do more. She began closing down website pages she'd been browsing when something occurred to her.

A few weeks ago, soon after she'd met Toby and uncovered the plot to misappropriate pedigree dogs,

Clarissa had googled Miranda Dervish. She'd been astonished to find zero results relating to the woman who had once claimed to be her aunt. But everything she'd tried to input into the search engine had yielded nil return.

Now she approached it a different way. The Sun Valley Pet Sanctuary had been closed down, and the manager of the kennels, an altogether unpleasant woman by the name of Sue Mitchelmore, had disappeared from the radar.

Sue Mitchelmore, under police questioning, had denied all knowledge of Miranda Dervish and had failed to identify her in the photographs DC Plum had shown her. With no evidence against her, Ed had no choice but to believe her story. Eventually, the police had dismissed even the hint of a charge against her.

But Clarissa wouldn't trust the ex-manager of the kennels as far as she could throw her.

Now, in an idle and tired moment, she googled Sue Mitchelmore's name rather than Miranda Dervish's. Several women came up in the search: an accountant on Facebook, a realty agent in California, a retired businesswoman on LinkedIn. None of these were of the slightest interest. Except in the photos.

Clarissa clicked through to Google Images, and there, amongst the lawyers and estate agents, the graduates and even a particularly scary-looking butcher, was a photo of 'her', Sue Mitchelmore. The candid shot had been taken by the *Sun Valley Tribune's* resident photographer, Terry Madeley.

Clarissa followed the link to the story. A Sun Valley Businesswoman of the Year award had been attended by numerous local dignitaries and high-flyers in the business world. Sue Mitchelmore had been there, and the photo had caught her raising a glass to the young winner, an enterprising dog-sitter who'd created an activity crèche for Sun Valley pooches.

All very nice.

Sue had been mingling as you'd expect with the beaming gathering of women, but one in particular stood out for Clarissa. Sue could be seen in the photo leaning sideways towards a smartly dressed friend, another woman, who'd placed a hand on Sue's shoulder and held her lips close to her ear, seemingly unaware of the camera pointed her way.

A tall woman with severe cheekbones and a razor-sharp bob.

A pointy woman.

Miranda Dervish.

CHAPTER SIX

Once upon a time, Temperance House had been owned by the local Quakers. When they'd decided to move on to more modern premises, their eighteenth-century building had rapidly fallen into disrepair. Abandoned for over a decade, the rundown stone premises with its leaking roof had been purchased by the Coven of the Silver Winds in the mid-1980s. The coven rapidly renovated it to something like its former glory, polishing the wooden floors and restoring the stained-glass windows.

Nestled between a pub on one side—ironically, given the Hall's name—and a bait and tackle shop on the other, Temperance House faced out onto the apron of Durscombe's busy harbour. Built from thick stone, it formed part of the sea wall on its rear side. During the season, tourists swarmed around the area, tucking into their fish and chips, licking their ice creams, or drinking the local scrumpy.

For the most part these innocent folk, so intent on having a good time, remained entirely oblivious to what went on within the walls of the pretty stone structure decorated with hanging plants and a sea-green wooden door. During the winter, the waves crashed into the back of the building with fierce intent, crashing over the roof and often showering anyone unfortunate enough to be strolling along the apron with a freezing salty spray.

The Coven of the Silver Winds had been established during the nineteenth century by a woman with an interesting—albeit dubious—reputation. Mary Mead had long been a member of a coven of some notoriety in London but, tiring of the increasing poverty and poor air of the capital, she'd decided to go it alone down in the south-west. A woman of both wealth and means—and the rumours were that she had gentlemen friends of high standing in business and banking who either fawned on her or gave into her blackmail demands when she had something on them—she had established a group of similar-minded male and female friends for congregational worship and ritual in East Devon. Upon her death in 1882, she had bequeathed her estate, and there was an awful lot of it, to the continued maintenance of the coven she had created and been so proud of.

Canny investment ensured that Temperance House and its endeavours had flourished until the current day.

Clarissa visited infrequently, certainly not as often as she probably should have done. However, she had always had an ambiguous relationship with her coven. Sheltered by her parents, she'd had no awareness of her heritage until, at the age of eight, Miranda Dervish had dumped her at Ravenswood Hall with the demand that she be inducted into the Coven of the Silver Winds when she turned seventeen.

And inducted she dutifully had been.

Educated to a decent standard at Ravenswood, and fully equipped to exist both in the witching and the mundane world, Clarissa had been doing perfectly alright. She preferred an existence without much need for magick. Living like normal people seemed so very soothing and calm. For the most part, her 'ordinary' friends lived fulfilling lives, entirely without drama.

And Clarissa appreciated the simple things in life.

However, she did enjoy the companionship and support of her brothers and sisters—many choosing to take the name Silverwind as their adopted surname, just as Old Joe had—and attended many of the most important rituals such as Samhain, Imbolc, Beltane and Lammas as the calendar dictated, along with any handfastings and solstice celebrations Temperance House hosted.

Occasionally, as today, Clarissa came to pore over the old volumes in the library. The library was rather a grand word to describe what was effectively a large cold room at the rear of the building. It housed three walls of towering shelving and one tiny barred window set high above your head. The infamous Bastille in Paris had probably never been as grim as this. Without a librarian or even a custodian of some description, the filing of the volumes, maps and archives was a little haphazard. A hit-and-miss card index offered the only search facility for users—although there were very few of them—to help visitors locate what they needed.

Clarissa dropped Toby's lead so he could wander around the room at will, dumped her bag on the table and retrieved her spectacles. The card index took the form of a large chest with many drawers, each of which snugly held blocks of cards measuring around six by four inches. Every card had been painstakingly hand-written and contained the author's name and title of book or document or subject name. It also gave a somewhat approximate location for you to begin your search.

Clarissa pulled open the drawer marked Ma-Mo, then hastily closed it again and instead searched through Da-Di. When she couldn't find anything relating to Miranda Dervish in the drawer, she returned to Ma-Mo and flicked through those cards too.

Nothing.

"No joy?" Toby asked, climbing up onto a seat at the large table in the centre of the room.

"There never seems to be where that woman is concerned, does there?" Clarissa swivelled slowly in place, surveying the shelves. "You'd think somewhere here, among all the books and the histories and the entries about individuals, there would be something about Miranda Dervish." She pulled a book off the shelf in front of her, glanced at the cover—it was an atlas of Europe in the sixteenth century—and shoved it back in its place.

"Is she a member of the Silver Winds coven?" Toby asked, and Clarissa stared at him as though he'd grown an extra head.

"Do you know? I hadn't thought of that." Clarissa frowned. "I'd assumed she was. I mean, because she went after Old Joe, but maybe she isn't."

"If she isn't, I suppose we won't find much here that relates to her at all."

"That's right. I'd have to visit the main archive at the Ministry of Witches in London, I suppose."

"Do they allow dogs in?"

Clarissa laughed. "I have no idea, but I don't see why not." She shuffled through the contents of a box on the shelf in front of her. It seemed to contain a mixture of recipes and written spells. Loose leaves from some departed witch's grimoire, no doubt.

Toby yawned and gave his head a quick shake. "Is it lunchtime yet?"

"We've only just arrived. Stop thinking about your stomach!"

Toby pouted. "It's not so much that I'm hungry as that I'd like my post-lunch nap."

Clarissa pointed at the floor. "Have a pre-lunch nap instead."

"I can't lie on that. It's rock hard and it's absolutely freezing in here!" Toby regarded the floor with some disdain. "They need some rugs."

"They could definitely do with some heating," Clarissa agreed. She rubbed her hands together, trying to warm them through. Outside the temperature was in the high sixties. It was a balmy day with brilliant blue skies and cotton wool clouds. In here, the temperature would have preserved dead bodies for weeks.

"If only these records were electronic." Clarissa

waved at the card index. "And they had a search engine."

"Can't you use Google Magick to speed things up? Then we can get out of here."

"Google Magick?" Clarissa queried. "Is there such a thing?"

Toby pointed with his paw at a large poster on the back of the door, partially obscured by someone's discarded robes.

It had the large colourful Google emblem and the word 'magick' underneath. "I thought you couldn't read?" Clarissa stepped closer and unhooked the robes so she could view the whole poster.

"I didn't think I could. But those are big words. I can see them and... I know what the letters are." Even Toby sounded surprised. "Can I read? I can, can't I?"

Clarissa turned about and eyed him thoughtfully. It seemed to her that his powers were growing almost daily. First he'd been able to talk, then he'd been able to discern images in photographs and now he could read words. Where would it end?

She looked back at the poster, and read aloud;

You are in a 13G frequency area.

To access Google Magick please follow these steps in turn:

1. First, locate the British Witchicom Hub.
2. Press reset and wait while the lights turn green. They will begin to flash.
3. If they don't flash, repeat step 2.
4. Wait until the lights on the British Witchicom Hub turn purple.
5. Direct your wand at the British Witchicom Hub.
6. Ask your question.
7. You should see results almost instantly, but please allow up to thirty seconds.
8. Repeat steps 2 through 7 as required.

"Well," Clarissa marvelled, "I never had anything like that at University."

"Do you have a wand?" Toby had never seen Clarissa use one.

"Mm. Somewhere." Clarissa's forehead creased as she reached for her bag. She knew it would be just her luck that she didn't have it with her. She rummaged at the bottom of her leather handbag. Toby had often thought her giant sack of a bag rather TARDIS-like. It seemed to hold such a vast array of items which, when pooled altogether in a heap on the floor, you'd never have imagined would fit inside such a confined space.

"Here it is. Right at the bottom with my biros."

Clarissa pulled out a handful of long thin items, several old scrappy tissues tangled around them. She pulled away the tissue, dropping the fragments on to the table, and then redeposited the pens in her bag, leaving only a slim length of worn wood.

"That's it?" Toby asked in surprise. "That doesn't look very powerful."

"It does the job," Clarissa replied. "To be fair, this is only a practice wand. They used to give these out at Ravenswood at the start of the year, the way they allocate textbooks. You're supposed to find your own wand, one that works for you, but so far, I've never even bothered looking."

She waved it gracefully in the air.

Tiny sparks glittered in the wand's wake.

Or it might just have been dust catching the light from the tiny barred window above their heads.

Nevertheless, Toby stared up at the wand in open-mouthed fascination. "Let's see what it can do," he said.

Clarissa searched around for the British Witchicom Hub and located it on top of a filing cabinet, slightly obscured by a pile of Deborah Harkness novels. She moved them out of the way and studied the Hub. The little light at the base glowed a steady orange. She pressed the button on top of the device and the light turned green and began to flash. Seconds later it turned a steady purple colour.

The air around them changed, became more electric. Something in the room seemed to buzz loudly. Toby twisted his head this way and that, searching for electric ions or bees or faeries or something else that might be causing the air to hum.

But it was magick that had brought the room to life.

And instantly, the chill in the room seemed to fall away too, as though someone had switched the heating on or lit a fire. The blood began to flow into Clarissa's fingers once more.

She lifted her wand. "Tell me about Miranda Dervish!"

Teeny, tiny sparks of light floated around above their heads, zipping here and there, around the shelves, above the shelves and below the shelves. They battered against boxes and settled on books, maps, rolls of parchment and sheaths of paper.

Then 99% of those sparks imploded, blinking out of existence.

A rattling thunking noise alerted Clarissa and Toby to a potential find, however. Toby jumped down from his chair and went straight to a heavy box on the bottom of a bookshelf. Sparks had formed an X on the front of the box, which rattled up and down, shaking in its confined space. As Toby reached it, the X exploded and evaporated with a whispering sigh.

Meanwhile, the light on the hub had turned orange and the zinging in the air had dissipated.

Clarissa clamped her wand between her teeth so she could use both hands, and dragged the box out from its place with some difficulty. Once she'd freed it enough, she lifted the lid. Inside were dozens and dozens of books. She pulled one out. The front looked familiar.

"Well I never," she smiled, sinking cross-legged to the floor, forgetting the chill, and placing her wand in her lap. "These are Ravenswood yearbooks."

Toby peered over her arm and sniffed at the slim volume she held in her hand. "What's a yearbook?"

"It's like a record of all the people in your school during one given year. It has photos of everyone and all their accomplishments, some information about the teachers and subjects. I'll be in here somewhere."

She returned the volume in her hand to the box and flicked through the ones at the front. "They're in year order and I left seven years ago... so... yes. Here we are."

She pulled the book out and opened it with a flourish, flicking through to find P for Page. She turned the book around to show Toby. She looked youthful, fresh-faced but with a large spot on her chin. Her hair had been longer. "Clarissa Louise Page. Coven of the Silver Winds."

"Cute." Toby wagged his tail. "Undeniably. And worth the giggle. But we asked about Miranda Dervish."

Clarissa closed the book and returned it to its place. "True. Does that mean she's in here, I wonder?"

She plucked her wand from her lap and tapped the side of the box. "Reveal your secrets," she demanded, and the books inside jostled together, rubbing against each other, until at last one seemed to sidle away from the others. Slowly, almost reluctantly, it rose an inch or so, sticking out above the rest.

Clarissa pulled the volume free and placed it on top of the box. It opened by itself, the pages turning over at speed until at last it remained still. Clarissa, with Toby by her side, scrutinised the page.

"Miranda Dervish," she read aloud. "And yes—see —it says here. Coven of the Silver Winds." They stared at the photograph of a young woman with long black hair and matching dark eyes. She didn't appear as slender at that age as she did now, not as pointy as he remembered from his recent encounter. Back then there'd been more flesh on her cheekbones and around her nose. However, with no hint of a smile, Toby recognised in the portrait's expression the merciless glare he'd seen her employ with Old Joe.

"When was this?" Toby asked.

Clarissa flipped the book so she could read the front cover. "1973."

"Is this the woman you remember?"

Clarissa nodded, a slow deliberate movement. This had been the woman who'd removed her from her home and transported her to Ravenswood. This was the woman on the CCTV at Sun Valley Pet Sanctuary.

"What about you?" Clarissa asked. "Is this her?"

Toby glowered at the page, holding back the snarl that bubbled in his throat.

Yes, this was The Pointy Woman.

This was the person who had killed Old Joe.

During the renovations of Temperance House, Mary Mead had used her foresight to incorporate a 'familiars hall'. This had been designed to act as a kind of cloakroom, but rather than deposit your coat—although you could if you wished—you deposited your familiar instead.

The Coven of the Silver Winds numbered several hundred souls spread across the globe. While most days there wouldn't have been more than a dozen local or visiting witches in situ, occasionally for the big celebrations, there could be scores of witches. Experience over the past fifty years had shown that if each of them brought a familiar along, this made for chaotic scenes in the ceremonial hall.

To that end, a room had been put aside specifically for furry and feathered companions and their ilk. The well-behaved among them were allowed to roam free. Those that were feral, or deadly in other ways, were required to be stored in a basket or cage.

Given this was Toby's first visit to Temperance House, he was taken aback when Clarissa opened the door to a room containing several cats, and by the smell of it, a rat in a cage too, and deposited him there.

"What's this?" he grumbled.

Clarissa took one look at his disgruntled face and decided to lie. "A canine crèche. I'd like to drop in on the High Priestess in the main hall and you can't come, so I need you to stay here for a little while."

Toby tried to back out. "Canine? But there are *cats* in here!"

"They won't hurt you." Clarissa guided him forwards, a firm push that brooked no argument.

"I might hurt them."

"Now be nice, Toby." She retreated to the door. "I'll be twenty minutes, max."

Toby huffed as she closed the door behind her, then turned about to glare at the other occupants of the room.

Whoever had designed the room had probably been responsible for the library too. Shelves lined the walls, but in this case only two walls. The wall opposite the dog faced out onto the harbour and had a large decorative window. Stained glass encased by wrought iron twirls. This was most effective at letting the light in, while keeping the curious stares of pedestrians out.

Arranged on the upper shelves were rows of colourful velvet cushions in jewel colours. One or two cats were curled up on these, snoozing peacefully. On the very top shelf, an owl twisted his head to look at Toby and hooed softly. Toby decided the hoot was welcoming.

The cages and baskets, for the most part, were tucked in on the bottom shelves. A blue-eyed husky regarded him with interest. Her snow-white snout turned up in a smile. "Hey," she said.

"Hi." Toby offered a small wag, wondering why she'd been caged, but deciding it might seem impertinent to ask. He continued looking around the room.

There were a pair of sofas in the centre of the room, each lorded over by a resident black cat.

Both of them turned an unblinking gaze his way.

Toby considered his options. He didn't want to appear as though he were scared of the cats, so he couldn't avoid them altogether. By the same token, he didn't want to seem uncool if he tried to clamber up to the cushions on the shelves above the crates and baskets. What if he fell? He supposed he could just find a place on the floor and curl up and wait patiently for Clarissa to return and save him from his own cowardice.

No.

What was he thinking? That would never do. No dog worth his salt would back down in a face-off with a cat, would they?

I'm a dog. Dogs are brave. Braver than cats. Nothing ventured, nothing gained.

Holding onto that thought, he sauntered over to the nearest sofa and leapt up, squidging himself carefully into the corner, cautious not to intrude on the cat's space.

"How do you do?" he asked the cat nearest to him in his best telephone voice. The kind he'd heard Old Joe adopt from time to time.

Her right ear twitched infinitesimally, and the irises in her eyes narrowed.

Toby continued unabashed. "I'm Toby."

She turned her head away.

"I belong to Clarissa Page. These days I do, at any rate. I used to belong to Joseph Silverwind." Toby looked across at the other cat sitting directly opposite. She appeared more interested in what he had to say. "Except back then I didn't know Old Joe was a witch. That was kind of a surprise."

The cat next to him shot him a look of such malevolence that Toby's insides began to shrivel up. He pulled his ears back anxiously.

"I'm sorry. Was it something I said?" he asked.

She rose, her head held at a haughty angle, and with an abrupt flick of her tail she hopped gracefully from the sofa, leaping in one swift movement up the shelves, and taking shelter on a bright red cushion at the very top. From there she glowered at Toby.

He blinked up at her.

"Ignore that jumped-up madam." The cat across the way studied the claws on her front paws. "She has a peculiarly inflated opinion of herself."

Toby dropped his attention to the opposite sofa. "Excuse me?"

"I said, ignore her. She thinks she's the Queen Bee."

Queen Bee? He could have sworn she was a cat. "And she isn't?" he asked, hesitant of taking sides when he didn't understand the dynamics at work here.

"Hell, no. She's a blessed puddy-tat like the rest of us. Her name is Jewel and she imagines she's a princess. And all because her Mama is Lady Jacqueline."

"Lady Jacqueline?" The name meant nothing to him. "Is she royalty?" This might explain the Queen Bee reference, Toby decided.

The cat twitched her whiskers. "Hardly, darling."

"Oh." Toby found himself struggling to understand the turn the conversation had taken.

"She's Jacqueline Naseby. Not a lady at all. That's just a term they use for second degree witches here."

Second degree witches? What?

The cat across from Toby giggled. "My. You're very green, aren't you boy?" She stood and stretched, and then hopped across the narrow chasm between them, sidling up to him to peer into his eyes. Her sleek black fur reflected the light and she smelled of grass and lavender and fresh laundry.

Toby liked the smell.

"I'm Juniper," she said.

"I'm—"

"Toby. I heard."

She weaved around his paws and then sank into an elegant sphinx-like pose next to him. "I belong to Geetha, one of the elders here."

"She's old?" Toby understood the term elder, or so he thought.

"She's not that old. Forty or so. But she's been a practising witch for a long time, and she knows her onions."

Toby considered burrowing his head beneath his paws. This all seemed so complicated to him. Who knew there were different kinds of onions? Old Joe used to make do with the brown ones from the supermarket. "She likes to garden?"

"She does as it happens. But that's not what I meant."

Juniper took a beat and then giggled. "Is it your first time here?"

"Is it that obvious?" Toby couldn't help but laugh a little too. He recognised how naïve he must sound to her.

"Just a bit." Juniper shifted and tucked her paws neatly underneath her body. "The way it works is that new witches are called neophytes. They study for a while, usually a year and a day, and are then initiated when they become first degree witches. Once they have intermediate knowledge of the craft, they can move on to become second degree witches. We use the term Lord and Lady here at the Coven of the Silver Winds."

"I see." Toby wondered what Clarissa was in the grand scheme of things. He wasn't sure she had a huge amount of practical magickal experience.

"A third-degree witch is most knowledgeable and will often act as a teacher or mentor to the neophytes, and if they're so inclined can become High Priest or High Priestess."

"And elders?"

"Elders are advanced practitioners. They may, as was the case with Joseph Silverwind, have been a High Priest or Priestess in their time, and retired from the position."

"You knew Joseph Silverwind?" Toby barked in surprise.

"Everybody knew Joseph Silverwind. He was a wonderful man. His death was a sad loss to the community."

From above their heads came a yowl. Jewel scowled down at them.

"Well, it's a sad loss to most of the Silver Wind

witches. I'm not sure Lady Jacqueline and Joseph the Elder were on particularly good terms."

"Is that right?" Toby asked, obviously interested in any enemies Joseph might have accrued within the confines of Temperance House.

"I believe he even petitioned to have Lady Jacqueline's status demoted at one time."

"Really?" Toby raised his head to consider the haughty Jewel high above his head, and this time when their eyes met, he returned her scowl with his own.

CHAPTER SEVEN

Clarissa, while a rare visitor to Temperance House, liked on occasion to make use of the facilities for her personal rituals. These included remembering her parents and politely requesting assistance from the specific gods and goddesses when she ran into a problem. Today she took the time to remember Joseph too.

It seemed incredible to her that she and Joseph might have unwittingly crossed paths here at Temperance House. Had he ever known she'd come here? Had he watched her here, knowing she was his granddaughter while she had no knowledge of his existence? She had no recollection of ever seeing him on the premises, but given what she knew, that he'd distanced himself from the Coven over the last few years, the timing suggested he'd resolutely kept his distance. He'd purposefully allowed her the freedom to continue with her life unhindered and unaware of his existence.

She finished up her ritual and extinguished the candles she'd been burning. She watched the wisps of smoke curl up and fade away, then bowed to the High Priestess before pattering across the varnished wood floor to the door. Outside, she retrieved her sandals and slipped them on, feeling at peace with the world, at least temporarily.

"Clarissa, isn't it?"

Clarissa, still bent over the buckle of her left shoe, glanced up. A woman of indeterminate age, the epitome of everything gothic, smiled down at her. She must have been in her late fifties, Clarissa guessed, with long lustrous hair dyed as black as a panther's coat, pale foundation applied thickly, and red lipstick.

"Yes." Clarissa straightened up.

"I'm Lady Jacqueline. I was a friend of Joseph Silverwind. A little birdie told me you're his granddaughter."

"They told you right," Clarissa replied.

"Well, that's astonishing. I wasn't aware he had a granddaughter. He never mentioned it to me."

Clarissa tilted her head, pondering how to respond to this, uncertain of the woman's motives. "We weren't close." She decided she wouldn't go into the details or admit to the fact that she would have loved to have been close to Joseph but had never enjoyed the opportunity.

"I see." The woman nodded and backed away. "Well, I wanted to pass on my commiserations. He was a great witch. Much admired."

Clarissa enjoyed hearing that. "Did you know him well?"

"Quite well. He was my mentor at one time." Lady Jacqueline continued to back away. "Anyway, I mustn't keep you. I'm sure you have things to do."

"Oh, not really." Clarissa's intentions had been to take Toby to the park, pick up some shopping and then head home to her laptop to make a start on one or two of the stories she intended to submit to magazines.

"Well, if you have the time, let's take tea?"

"That sounds like a great idea." Clarissa had begun to warm to Lady Jacqueline. She had a pleasant open smile and incredibly white teeth. "But I'll have to retrieve my purse. I've left it in my bag." She indicated the Hall of Familiars.

"Don't be silly. It's my treat." She indicated the staircase ahead of them and Clarissa followed her up. Lady Jacqueline wore long black robes, and seemed to float as she climbed the stairs.

Temperance House accommodated a tearoom on

the mezzanine level, more or less directly above the hall of familiars. At certain times of the year, at summer solstice and Samhain, for example, caterers were employed to facilitate the feasting required. For the rest of the year, a solitary tea lady named Shirley brought in cakes she'd baked at home, and conjured up egg and cress sandwiches, Devon Cream Teas and pots of tea on demand.

Clarissa joined Lady Jacqueline at a table by the window. It overlooked the busy harbour. The tide was out and the boats that hadn't set out for sea this morning lay marooned, leaning dramatically to one side, awaiting the moment the waters would stream back in and float them to freedom once more. Tourists and sightseers pottered around, staring into gift shop windows, poring over the fish on display at the fishmongers, or studying the cost of entry to the aquarium.

Clarissa ordered tea and a slice of Victoria sponge. Lunchtime wasn't far away and she could have eaten a sandwich, but she'd promised Toby she'd only be twenty minutes. She could imagine the kerfuffle he'd raise if she stayed away too long, and consumed an egg and cress sandwich to boot.

She smiled, thinking of him fondly. No doubt once she'd confessed to such a misdemeanour, egg and cress would be today's favourite favourite.

But the cake was a welcome treat. She cut into it with a dessert fork and marvelled at its light, crumbly texture. Clarissa had taken some home economics classes at Ravenswood, but once she'd headed off to University she had survived on pasta, pizza and stir fry.

"You were saying you didn't have much of a relationship with Joseph?" Lady Jacqueline enquired. She'd settled for a glass of mint tea. She smiled at Clarissa over the sugar-coated rim of her glass.

"I didn't know him." Clarissa remained guarded, not sure how much or what to share.

"That's such a shame. It's always nice to have contact with your grandparents." Lady Jacqueline sipped at her tea.

"Tell me what he was like?" Clarissa asked. "I'd love to know more about him."

"Oooh. Now you're putting me on the spot." Lady Jacqueline replaced her glass and straightened the small handbag she'd left by the side of the saucer. Perhaps she was taking the time to think about her answer. When she looked up at Clarissa, the jovial, relaxed expression on her face had disappeared. Her eyes could have cut glass.

"He was a difficult man," she announced.

Clarissa rocked back slightly on her chair and

raised her eyebrows. This wasn't what she'd been expecting to hear. "In what way?"

"Obstreperous."

"Obstreperous?" Clarissa repeated.

"He could be argumentative, particularly during meetings of the Council of Elders. He often disagreed with the way things were being run and he didn't hold back from making his feelings known."

"He was a man of strong opinions?" Clarissa interpreted the other woman's words.

"Oh, most definitely. He knew what he wanted and if he couldn't get his way, he could be abrasive."

Clarissa puzzled over Lady Jacqueline's words. She'd never heard it said by anyone else that Old Joe had been abrasive.

"I'd heard he hadn't been particularly active with the coven or attended many meetings in recent years." Wasn't that what Catesby had told her the last time she'd seen her at Ravenswood?

"Well…" Lady Jacqueline dabbed delicately at the corners of her mouth with the napkin. "It's not so much that he wasn't active, as that the High Priest asked him to stay away."

"You're kidding?" Clarissa couldn't quite believe what she was hearing. You had to behave really badly to be asked to leave a coven. Most forms of behaviour, regardless of what they were, while not welcomed exactly, were tolerated. Magick took many forms after all, and witches, like 'normal' people generally, have their flaws.

Covens tended to avoid being judgmental. But the Coven of the Silver Winds had practically banished Joseph by the sound of it. That would explain why Toby had been unaware of Old Joe ever attending Temperance House, or even of being a practising witch.

"You know," Lady Jacqueline leaned over her mint tea and lowered her voice, "Joseph could be incredibly rude. He upset people in high places, I'm given to understand."

Clarissa, confused by the revelation, drew in her breath. "Is that what got him killed, do you think?"

"Killed?" Lady Jacqueline raised her perfectly plucked eyebrows. "I'd heard he died of natural causes."

Clarissa stopped herself from correcting the other woman but held her gaze nonetheless, subconsciously scanning her face, seeking some truth about Old Joe and who he'd been.

Lady Jacqueline leaned back in her seat and

regarded Clarissa through hooded eyes. "The police aren't investigating it as murder, are they?"

Clarissa broke off another piece of cake and raised it to her lips, busying herself with something—anything—to cover the confusion she was feeling. "No, they're not." She settled for the truth and no more.

Lady Jacqueline nodded. "There's no evidence, then? Not for anything other than natural causes?"

Clarissa avoided her eyes. "That's right."

"Even so, it must be terrible for you."

"Yes." Clarissa nibbled on her cake.

"Oh my dear, you look perfectly miserable. I'm so sorry, I hope I didn't say anything out of turn."

"No, no," Clarissa reassured her, looking up and forcing a smile. "It's always better to hear an honest opinion."

"Well, there is that. And of course, I can't deny that your grandfather was a magnificent witch. So incredibly talented. He made for a wonderful mentor and taught many young neophytes a wide range of skills in his time here."

So what changed? Clarissa wondered. *Why did he fall out with the Coven of the Silver Winds so spectacularly?*

"Anyway, it is lovely to have you here at Temperance House. I hope you'll visit us more often."

"I'll certainly try," Clarissa replied. *After all, I've just lost my job so I have plenty more time on my hands.*

"And if there's anything you need, anything at all, I'd be happy to assist. You know the High Priestess is considering granting me a role as an Elder. You can trust me." She reached into her slim clasp handbag and extracted her purse. She waved a ten-pound note at Shirley, who dutifully trotted over with some change.

Lady Jacqueline waved the coins away.

"And if you ever need a sympathetic ear, I'd be more than happy to listen." She plucked a business card from her purse and handed it over to Clarissa.

Clarissa studied the front. A photo of Lady Jacqueline in full-on gothic make-up and the words, *Lady Jacqueline. Mystic and clairvoyant.* Her phone number and email address were recorded on the reverse.

"But you can usually find me hanging around here somewhere," Lady Jacqueline twinkled.

As Clarissa rose, the older woman held a hand up. "It must be difficult for you to live in the same house where Joseph died."

Clarissa stared at her in surprise. She hadn't mentioned where she was living.

"All that unresolved trauma," Lady Jacqueline continued. "Perhaps you need to exorcise the spirits."

"No, it's fine," Clarissa told her. "If there is trauma, we're working at resolving it."

"We?"

"My dog and I."

"Would that be Joseph's dog?" Lady Jacqueline asked, her tone light and breezy, but her words carrying some weight.

Clarissa shifted uneasily.

She supposed that being a clairvoyant and mystic might have something to do with what Lady Jacqueline knew, but even so, her questions were too personal for comfort. She chose not to answer the question but instead asked one of her own. "Do you know Miranda Dervish?"

"Miranda Dervish?" Lady Jacqueline's eyes glittered, but they no longer contained even a modicum of warmth or cheer. "No, I don't think I've ever heard of her."

Clarissa smiled with as much warmth as she could muster. "Oh. My mistake." She shrugged as though it didn't matter at all. "It was a long shot. Ignore me."

She wiggled her fingers goodbye, knowing without a shadow of a doubt that Lady Jacqueline was lying through her straight white teeth.

"Hey?" Clarissa rushed into the Hall of Familiars and grabbed her rucksack. "Are you ready?" she asked Toby.

"I sure am." He jumped down from his sofa. "Farewell Juniper. It's been enlightening chatting with you."

Juniper winked at him. "Don't be a stranger."

Clarissa clipped his lead onto his collar and hustled him out of the room, closing the door behind her and then rummaging in her rucksack for her purse so that she could store Lady Jacqueline's card for future reference. "Did you make a friend?"

"I most certainly did, and we really need to talk—"

"Clarissa?" An authoritative voice stopped them dead in their tracks. Clarissa glanced up from where she was fiddling with a zip. She straightened immediately. The High Priestess. Lady Amphitrite, named after the Greek goddess of the sea. Fitting, here on the coast. Remarkably young and relatively new to the position as head of the coven, she nevertheless had the charisma and aura to carry it off. "Would it be possible to have a quick word?"

"Of course!" Clarissa gestured at her bag and Toby. "I'll just—"

"No need. Leave them there. I really won't keep you very long."

"Yes, my lady." Clarissa dropped Toby's lead and wagged a finger at him. *Behave*, she mouthed.

He flicked his ears. As if he'd do anything else.

Clarissa trotted after Lady Amphitrite. The High Priestess had a small office on the opposite side of the entrance hall to the ceremonial room. Part office, part study, there was a large desk and two comfortable leather armchairs on either side of a fire. No fire burned in the grate today. There was no need on such a warm day as this.

Lady Amphitrite indicated Clarissa take a seat. "I'll get straight to the point, Clarissa." She picked up a sheet of paper from the desk and then sat opposite the young journalist. "We're delighted that you've chosen to be more active in the Coven of the Silver Winds of course—"

By that, she probably meant that it was nice of Clarissa to finally turn up after months of non-activity. Clarissa grimaced, guilt a hard stone in the pit of her stomach.

"Don't get me wrong. How often or how little you attend congregation is entirely up to you, and we set no limits on any individual." Lady Amphitrite studied Clarissa's face. "However, it has come to our attention that you have brought the Coven of the Silver Winds into disrepute."

"Disrepute?" Clarissa sat bolt upright. There was that word again. "I don't think I have."

Lady Amphitrite waved the sheet of paper. "As you know, I lead this Coven, and I have pledged an oath to do so to the best of my ability. I make the day-to-day decisions about how we run things here. However, I am led in part by the coven's Council of Elders, and they have today written to me with instructions. It is their decision to dispel you from our circle."

"You want to banish me?" Clarissa's voice rose in shock.

"It is the Council of Elders' decision," Lady Amphitrite reiterated. "I personally have no bones with you."

Clarissa dug her fingers into her knees. "A decision based on what? How have I brought the coven into disrepute?"

Lady Amphitrite studied the letter in her hand. "By hounding another member of the coven."

Clarissa blinked. "Who?

"I'm afraid I'm not at liberty to say." The High Priestess remained smooth and unemotional. She was only performing her duties as they had been laid out by the Council of Elders.

Clarissa bristled. "How very convenient." This wasn't rocket science. She didn't need confirmation of a name. She could guess. Forty or fifty minutes ago she had been downstairs in the library asking Google Magick to spill the beans on Miranda Dervish. If she hadn't been side-tracked by Lady Jacqueline, she would have already left Temperance House and this letter would not have had the time to materialise.

She'd been waylaid on purpose.

Something here stank to high heaven.

"There are of course appeal procedures that you can pursue, if you wish."

"I do wish." Clarissa's body shook with pent-up anxiety and rage. Every way she turned, Miranda Dervish appeared to be intent on ruining her life. First Old Joe. Then Mrs Crouch. Then her job and now finally, her coven too. She had no intention of taking this lying down. She jumped to her feet and through gritted teeth managed to add, "I'll fight it all the way. Good day to you, Lady Amphitrite."

"Could you just slow down?" Toby asked. Clarissa was taking such long strides he was struggling to keep up with her. And besides, after spending nearly two hours cooped up in Temperance House, he badly needed to cock a leg somewhere.

"Sorry." Clarissa pulled up and let him investigate the lamppost next to them. Her features were creased, the set of her face thunderous.

"What's up?" Toby asked, slipping closer and nudging her hand. "You're upset."

"You're not kidding," Clarissa griped, and pulled on the lead as they resumed walking once more.

"Do you want to share?" Toby asked, trotting with her, anxious to reach inside her prickly defence.

She halted again and turned to face him, tears springing into her eyes. "It's Miranda Dervish. I swear she's trying to wreck our lives."

Toby nodded. "Go on."

"Well it goes without saying, doesn't it? Old Joe and Mrs Crouch?"

"Yes." Toby sat squarely at her feet and waited for her to say more.

"Then I'm fired from the job I love and I'm pretty certain she was behind that."

"Agreed," said Toby, and the tip of his tail wagged in encouragement.

"And now I've been ejected from the coven for hounding another member."

"Ejected?"

"Banished. Asked not to come back." Clarissa fluttered her hands at her eyes. "And we can only guess at the member I'm supposed to have hounded."

"That would only be Miranda Dervish," Toby finished for her.

"Precisely." Tears rolled down Clarissa's face. "I swear she won't stop until she's destroyed us."

At that, Toby leapt up and patted his paws against Clarissa's thighs. "We won't let that happen!"

"It all feels like everything is out of our control right now." Clarissa rubbed at her eyes, then knelt down to pull the dog into her arms.

He licked her face then stepped back so he could look at her properly. "We have to beat her at her own game."

Clarissa sniffed. "How do you propose we do that, Mr Clever Clogs?"

Toby wagged his tail harder. "Elementary, my dear Clarissa. We take a closer look at her background, starting with the yearbook."

Clarissa glanced back the way they'd come, down to the harbour. "But I can't go back there. I'm barred, pending appeal."

Toby barked in excitement, and danced round in a circle, before jumping up at her again. "It's a good job I returned to the library and dug out her yearbook then, isn't it? It's in your rucksack."

"You did what?" Clarissa couldn't believe her ears. "That's stealing!"

"I borrowed it. That's what libraries are for."

"You shouldn't have."

"You were too busy having your wrists slapped by the High Priestess to notice," Toby shrugged. "It's a good starting point. We need to work out where she went after Ravenswood and take it from there."

"Agreed."

"We also know that she killed Old Joe and attacked Mrs Crouch because she was after the gemstones. If we can figure out what the stones are for, maybe we'll be a step closer to knowing why The Pointy Woman wants them and where we can find her."

"That's true." A good idea, thought Clarissa. "But where do we start?"

"Who else might know something about the stones?" Toby asked. "Besides Mrs Crouch? She's still poorly."

"Yes, she is." Clarissa remembered the pile of clippings they'd found under the bed. "Maybe we could go and look at her photos and notebook again. Perhaps there's something in there that will help us understand what the stones are for and why Mrs Crouch has one."

"I thought you'd ruled out looking through Mrs Crouch's personal effects?"

"I had," replied Clarissa. "But desperate times call for desperate measures."

CHAPTER EIGHT

Clarissa removed her spectacles and rubbed her face. The glare from the laptop had started to irritate her eyes, and she blinked into the distance at Toby who lay fast asleep in his basket, one leg as usual pointing at the ceiling.

She stretched her spine out, feeling the click as something uncramped in her neck, then surveyed her desk. Paper, notebooks, pens and post-its littered the area, with still more to look through. She didn't seem to be getting anywhere fast. She'd unearthed no reference to the gemstones, and nothing about Miranda Dervish. She still had plenty more research to do though, if not the energy to continue this evening.

She briefly considered more coffee, but this close to bedtime it probably wouldn't be a good idea. Instead, she stood and picked up her mug, intending to run herself a glass of water from the tap and check on Toby's water bowl.

He stirred as she pushed her chair back.

"Is it dinner time?" he asked.

Clarissa squinted at him. "I could have sworn we ate just a couple of hours ago."

"Did we?" Toby righted himself and yawned. "I'd forgotten." He peered up at her hopefully. "Walkies then?"

Clarissa bent down to check the time on her laptop. A quarter to nine or nearabouts. She should really take him for a quick shuffle round the block. Her eye fell on the manila folder she'd retrieved from Mrs Crouch's bedroom, and she regarded it with an element of guilt and misgiving. Hoping her elderly neighbour might have recovered somewhat and saved her the trouble of simply taking the folder without asking, she'd popped over to the hospital earlier this afternoon, but Mrs Crouch remained in the intensive care unit and the nurses wouldn't allow Clarissa to see her. Close family only, they'd told her.

But where were Mrs Crouch's close family, if indeed she had any?

The good news was that Mrs Crouch hadn't deteriorated any further. There had been no change in her condition at all, but she hadn't woken up, and Clarissa could tell that everyone was worried about her.

Unable to ask permission from her neighbour to read the folder's contents, Clarissa had headed back to Chamberlain Drive and let herself back into Mrs Crouch's house while Toby stood guard outside. He wasn't much good as security, given that he tended to be a little wimpy—which in itself was understandable of course—but he could at least raise the alarm if anyone approached while Clarissa was inside.

She hadn't hung around, simply made her way upstairs and pulled out the suitcases to extract the folder. She'd brought it home and placed it on her desk, where it had remained ever since.

The yearbook Toby had 'borrowed' from Temperance House had not yielded any obvious clues. Clarissa had flicked through page after page, scanning the contents. The annual intake at Ravenswood had been even smaller in Miranda Dervish's day than in Clarissa's. Her year group had numbered around sixty. Miranda had thirty-four classmates, including one Grace Catesby.

Clarissa hadn't realised the two women were contemporaries. She wondered what bonds had formed between them. What vows had been spoken?

Which blood rituals had they undertaken? Had they pledged to be sisters for life?

For the most part, Clarissa had remained an outsider at Ravenswood. She'd had a couple of close friends, both of whom she had continued to keep in touch with for a little while. Now, although they had drifted apart once they'd headed their separate ways to University, she understood if she were ever in a fix, they would be the first people she could call.

"Yes. We ought to have a quick walk," Clarissa told Toby. He wagged his tail and trotted through to the kitchen to wait for Clarissa at the back door.

Clarissa threw her spectacles onto the table, intending to follow him out. Her aim was poor. The manila folder, already perched precariously on the full table, tipped over the edge and spilled its contents over the floor.

"For Pete's sake," Clarissa muttered and bent down to retrieve them.

Toby trotted out from the kitchen. "Who's Pete?"

Clarissa smiled at his curiosity. "To be honest, I have no idea. I don't think I know any Petes."

"Why do we need to worry about doing something for his sake, then?" Toby cocked his head.

"You can be very literal at times." Clarissa scooped up the newspaper cuttings, letters and photos and the notebook from the floor and pushed them back inside the manila folder. But the photo on top caught her eye.

"Ha. We should drop this folder more often. Look at this lady. She seems familiar…" Clarissa flipped the photo over. "Yes. The name rings a bell too."

She placed the photograph on the floor in front of her and reached up to the table for the yearbook.

Toby studied the photo. "It's from a long time ago."

"For some people the 1970s really aren't that long ago, I imagine." Clarissa thumbed through the yearbook. "Here we are. 'Mabel 'the Magnificent' Armistead', it says here. Class of 1966 to 1973. She studied at Ravenswood at more or less the same time as Miranda."

"Mabel Armistead?" repeated Toby. "I met a Mabel once."

"Armistead?" Clarissa asked.

Toby screwed up his eyes, trying to remember. "I can't remember."

"Did she look anything like this? A bit older obviously?"

Toby studied the photograph with renewed interest. "I can't be sure," he announced finally. "The Mabel I met was bonkers."

"Bonkers?"

"As mad as a hatter."

"Toby!" Clarissa reprimanded him. You can't say that."

"I can." Toby regarded Clarissa with surprise. "Ever since The Pointy Woman gave me the ability, I've been able to say many things."

"I meant, it isn't nice to say such things of people."

"Oh." Toby didn't understand the niceties of human behaviour at times. "Well she was… that word."

Clarissa pulled a face. "In what way?"

"She looked like a scarecrow. And I think she was scared. Old Joe gave her some money—"

"Wait. She knew Old Joe?"

"It certainly seemed that way. They were like old friends. She came to the door in the dead of night. Old Joe must have been expecting her."

"What makes you say that?"

Toby thought back, remembering Old Joe's strange behaviour that night. "He removed the bulb from the front light. The one that's supposed to come on when anyone approaches the house. I thought that was strange because it was working, but he got the stepladder out of the shed and he went up there by himself, even though I told him he shouldn't. He was an old man—"

Toby remembered Old Joe falling to the floor after The Pointy Woman had tripped him with her handbag and the sound his breaking bones had made, and shuddered.

"I told him not to, but he did it anyway," Toby repeated, his soft voice was a lament for his beloved owner.

Clarissa reached out and fondled his ears. "And then?"

"He stayed up that night. Much later than normal. I've told you before, he used to tire easily, so we would tuck ourselves up for the night quite early. He might watch a little bit of the ten o'clock news, but then he'd take a hot chocolate or a cup of tea up to bed and pretend to read for a little while. Invariably the drink would go cold and he wouldn't read more than a page."

"But not that night?"

"No. That night he sat up. I stayed with him. He turned the television off and we sat in silence until he said, 'We're going to have a visitor any second, Toby. Don't bark at her'. That's what he said. And then maybe twenty seconds later I heard a scratching at the door and Old Joe went and let her in."

"So why did you think she was 'bonkers'?" Clarissa asked.

"Well, for one thing the way she was dressed and what she looked like, and for another because she turned up at a stupid time in the morning when Old Joe should have been asleep."

Clarissa rolled her eyes. "How was she dressed?"

Toby looked down at the photograph of a woman in her twenties or early thirties with neatly curled short hair and a pleasant smile. "Not like that. More like a hedge."

"You mean like someone who'd been dragged through a hedge?"

Toby stuck to his guns. "No, I mean like a hedge."

Clarissa conceded she was getting nowhere. "So what did this Mabel want?"

"Money."

"And did Old Joe give it to her?"

"He did. I remember he asked her what she'd done with the rest and she said she'd had an emergency and it was all gone. He told her he would send her more next month."

This news gave Clarissa pause. "And when was this?"

"It would have been three or four months before he... before he died."

Clarissa stood up and tapped her mouse, re-activating the laptop which had gone dark through inactivity.

"Can we go out now? I badly need to do my thing."

Clarissa had slipped back into her chair. "Toby, be a darling and just go in the garden, can you? I promise we'll have a long walk in the morning."

Toby stretched his head up to look at the computer screen as Clarissa started tapping away at the keyboard. "What are you doing?"

"I'm going to look at Old Joe's banking records. The solicitor gave me access so I could sort out final payments and stop the standing orders and the like. I want to see if Old Joe sent a payment to a Mabel and then we'll be able to find her surname. See if it's the same one as in the photograph."

"Armistead?" Toby remembered.

"Exactly." Clarissa opened up a group of PDF documents and started scrolling through them. Old Joe hadn't really spent much money at all. There were transactions at the supermarket and the local shops, payment to energy companies, and for rates and his television licence, so anything besides the obvious stood out a mile.

"Here." Clarissa leaned into the screen. "A payment of five hundred pounds to Mabel Armistead. Well I'm blowed."

Toby regarded Clarissa doubtfully. He couldn't feel a draught or a breeze so he wasn't sure how Clarissa could be blowed, but she appeared jubilant about something. He danced in place, partly with happiness, partly because he needed to visit the little dog's room outside.

"Does that mean you'll be able to track her down?" Toby asked.

Clarissa shook her head. "There's no address here. It just says account payee is one Mabel Armistead. And you're right, this was about nine months ago."

"I'm not sure how that helps us."

"Well, it just proves that she exists. That's not bad for starters. I mean, we haven't had much luck so far." Clarissa swung back in her chair and threw her arms into the air, stretching rather majestically and then steepling her fingers and placing her hands on top of her head. "And think about it, Toby. This proves a link between Old Joe, Mrs Crouch—because she has a photo of the young Mabel after all—and The Pointy Woman, because Mabel and Miranda are in the same yearbook and knew each other at Ravenswood."

Clarissa blew her breath out hard. "Exciting!"

"I suppose so." Toby was less enthused.

"Now if only we could find her and have a chat, we might finally be part of the way to solving the riddle of the stones. Wouldn't that be great?" Clarissa tipped forward once more, flexing her fingers above the keyboard. "But where do we start looking for her?"

Toby, realising Clarissa wasn't up for a jaunt around the block, accepted that he'd have to make do with the garden. He turned huffily and pitter-pattered out into the hall. "I told you," he called back. "You'll find her in a hedge."

CHAPTER NINE

"Where are we?" Toby sat up and glanced out of the car window. His stomach rolled a little. He hadn't yet become accustomed to riding in a car, and travel sickness put him off practising. Clarissa seemed an able driver, if a little uncomplimentary when it came to other road users.

"Look at that old dear," she would grumble. "She can barely see above the steering wheel *and* she's driving with her mirrors tucked in. What if someone wants to overtake her?"

Toby's ears twitched and his stomach twinged just thinking about someone trying to overtake anyone on these narrow, winding roads. Clarissa's old Nissan car had no air-conditioning, and in this warm weather they'd been enjoying, she liked to drive with the windows down. If Toby stuck his head out of the passenger window he often got more than he bargained for, so close did Clarissa have to drive to the hedgerows and verges.

Instead, he curled up in a ball and closed his eyes, willing the journey to be over.

But now they had pulled up and Clarissa had killed the engine. Toby sat up and took in his surroundings. Nothing very exciting. A car park. Lots of cars and a few people wandering around looking lost.

"I think we were lucky to find a parking spot," Clarissa said, rummaging around in her big sack-like leather bag for her purse. "Now, do I have any change?"

She opened the door and Toby smelt the seaside. "Where are we?"

"We're in a little town called Beer." Clarissa unzipped her coin purse and grunted as she fingered the contents.

"Beer? As in the drink?"

"Yes. Wait here a sec, will you? I'll go and grab a ticket."

Toby watched Clarissa weave through the cars towards a ticket machine. "Old Joe liked beer," he remembered. They had on occasion sat out in a beer garden and shared a bag of salt and vinegar crisps while Old Joe supped a pint, usually with a great deal of satisfaction. "I wonder if beer comes from Beer."

"Right!" Clarissa had returned. She slipped a small piece of paper onto the dashboard and reached for Toby's lead. "Ready?"

"Do you know where we're going?" Toby jumped out of the car, pleased to breathe the fresh sea air.

"I have a vague idea." Clarissa led the way out of the car park. "We need to head slightly away from the town centre, and dip down towards the sea. I had a look on Google maps this morning and I didn't really fancy driving down the lane here, or trying to find somewhere to park—"

"So you found Mad Mabel's address?"

"Please don't call her that!" Clarissa shot Toby a sharp look. "Especially in her presence."

Toby raised his thick eyebrows. "Well, did you? Find an address?"

"Not exactly. I found several references in the local newspaper, various dates over the past thirty years, and several of the older ones reference her as living at Scavenger Cottage. Needless to say, there aren't many cottages with that name so I'm going to assume I have the right one. Whether she lives there or not, we'll soon find out."

Somewhere high above their heads, the summer sun tried to find a way to filter through the layer of cloud. The overcast day made everything more humid than was pleasant, and Clarissa dabbed at her forehead with the back of her hand and blew her fringe out of her eyes as they began to descend a steep incline.

"This is a road?" Toby asked. The total width of the lane was approximately seven feet. Weeds grew up through the tarmac in the middle.

"Apparently so. Now you can see why I decided not to drive down it."

Toby trotted alongside Clarissa, taking in the smells. The sea couldn't be far away, and the verges had been frequented by walkers and their dogs, as well as neighbourhood cats and a variety of typical wildlife, foxes, badgers and squirrels. *Mm-mm, enticing*, thought Toby, wishing he had more time to explore.

"Phew. It's a tad warm." Clarissa stopped for a breather and checked to her left. A narrow entranceway led to a tangled jungle of a garden. "Is this it?"

She pushed into the narrow gap that might once have been a path, but now was simply a slightly less overgrown area than anywhere else. A rusted gate, completely off its hinges, had been engulfed by the overgrowth.

"It's not looking good," Clarissa said, her eyes narrowing in the direction of the ramshackle cottage up ahead. From their current vantage point she could see the top storey and the slightly sagging roof. One or two slates had slipped or were missing altogether, the lichen grew thick elsewhere, and the iron guttering had come loose above one of the windows. The single-glazed windows had wooden frames, badly in need of painting. If this humble building was indeed Scavenger Cottage, it needed a great deal of work.

"Let's investigate!" Toby pulled at the lead, so Clarissa bent down to unclip him.

"Don't chase anything," she warned him. "And watch out for traps and things."

"It's a garden, not the Wild West," Toby called back as he raced off and began exploring, dodging underneath the bushiest of rose bushes and clingiest of climbers.

Clarissa followed at a more sedate pace, picking her way carefully between Jurassic garden plants. Some of the ferns in this garden were the tallest she had ever seen. A walk in this garden had you feeling like you were Gulliver on his travels.

The scent of good earth was heavy in the air, along with the light, sweet lemon scent of summer foliage, combined with an edge of pepper. Brambles and rose thorns grabbed at her t-shirt and scratched her bare arms. Tiny flies buzzed annoyingly around her head.

She swatted them away with the map printout she still held in her sweaty hand.

"Over here," Toby called, and she followed the sound of his excited bark down a series of steps, hewn roughly from stone, that led to an open door. A little wooden plaque at head height, hand-painted in dark blue letters, announced they had indeed located Scavenger Cottage.

Toby waited patiently at the door for Clarissa to join him.

"Is anyone in?" Clarissa, doubtful, cast an eye about.

Weeds grew through the patio paving here, and a bath, half-filled with stagnant water, appeared to have attracted numerous frogs and dragonflies. Graffiti had been sprayed on the wall near the door, and the door itself appeared to have been kicked in. The lock had long been broken by the look of things; the splintering around it had weathered over time.

Mabel Armistead could not possibly be inhabiting this place.

"Hello?" Clarissa called.

An answering yowl had them both shuffling backwards. A slender black cat stalked into view and levelled them both with blazing eyes, her hair bristling, her tail pointing straight up. Scrawny and obviously elderly, her shoulder blades jutted through her fur, and the skin at her throat hung loose. She probably hadn't enjoyed a decent meal in weeks.

"You're not welcome here," she spat at Toby, as though that hadn't immediately been obvious the second she'd clapped eyes on them.

"I beg your pardon, Madam." Toby sat neatly on the doorstep. "I hope we didn't alarm you."

"What did she say?" Clarissa asked. "Can you understand what she says?"

Toby glanced up at Clarissa. "Shh." He turned back to the cat. "I apologise for my hooman. She doesn't speak any animal tongues."

The cat blinked at Clarissa. "But she understands what you say?"

"I was hexed. It's a long story. It's partly why we're here. We're looking for the woman who killed my previous hooman."

"You won't find her here." The cat glared at him. "You won't find anyone here. Best you just go back to where you came from."

"We're looking for Mabel." Toby tried again. "If you know where we can find her, we'd have a quick word and be on our way."

"Mabel didn't kill your human. Mabel wouldn't

hurt a fly." The cat coughed and hawked. Toby grimaced. She didn't sound at all well.

"What are you two talking about?" Clarissa asked impatiently, wafting away another irritating cloud of gnats. "Is Mabel here?"

"If she isn't here, where is she?" Toby kept his tone light and pleasant. He wanted the cat to understand they meant no harm to anyone.

"Maybe she's dead." The cat regarded Toby through troubled eyes. "Had you thought of that?"

"Is she?" He had thought of it.

"Could we come in and get a glass of water or something?" Clarissa stepped forward. Her encroachment on the cat's personal space proved to be a red rag to a bull. The cat screeched and arched her back, hissing and spitting at the young witch.

Clarissa lifted her hands and stepped back. "Peace out, kitty."

Toby's head swivelled between the cat and Clarissa and back again. He apologised once more. "I'm really sorry about her. It's a very hot day. She doesn't regulate her temperature very well at all."

With one final hiss at Clarissa, the cat nodded at Toby. "I told you. You should leave."

"When was the last time you had something to

eat?" asked Toby, ignoring her instruction. "Or drink? Do you like sammiches? I like sammiches."

The cat sniffed in disdain, as though the idea of sustenance was below her.

Toby refused to give up. "What about tuna sammiches? Do you like them?"

The cat blinked. Once. Twice. "I do like tuna," she replied.

"Oh wow! Tuna's my favourite too! My favourite favourite."

Twenty-five minutes later Clarissa, hotter and sweatier than ever, returned with a bag of shopping. She'd hiked up the steep hill back into town and located a mini supermarket. Inside she'd purchased a number of sandwiches, a carton of milk, a few bottles of water and three tins of tuna.

She puffed along the path towards Scavenger Cottage. "I come bearing gifts," she said when she spotted Toby. He lay half-in and half-out of the shadow of the house. The cat maintained her previous defensive position, blocking entrance through the door.

"At last." Toby scrambled to his feet. "We were about to die of starvation."

"Hush you." Clarissa's eyebrows drew together as she regarded the cat. Toby certainly wasn't in any danger of going hungry. The cat was a different story. She emptied the bag and showed them the sandwiches. Peeling back the cellophane wrapper from one, she broke a chunk off for Toby and handed it to him. He devoured it instantly.

Clarissa broke off a smaller piece for the cat and held it out.

The cat remained where she was. She didn't move so much as a whisker. That had to take some willpower.

Clarissa gently threw the chunk of sandwich towards the cat. It landed between the cat's front paws. She glanced down at it, then sniffed it. Tentatively, she stuck out her tongue and licked at one edge. She seemed to like the tuna, and the spread inside, but not the bread.

Clarissa held up a can of tuna. "I don't have a tin opener, but I bet you have one in the kitchen? If you let us in I can fill your bowl for you."

The cat turned her green eyes on Toby once more. "Is this some kind of trick?"

"Not at all," Toby reassured her, wagging his tail.

"Clarissa is a good hooman. She likes to feed everyone."

The cat glared up at Clarissa for a long moment, studying her face, considering her intentions. Toby imagined that, given the haughty set of her head, she would continue to rebuff them, but suddenly, without warning, her defences seemed to crumble. In their place he saw only a tired, old cat, down on her luck and desperate for food.

She pushed herself upright, her back legs stiff with age, and ambled away from the door, giving Toby and Clarissa access.

They followed her into the kitchen, slowly and respectfully, mindful of what it had taken for her to back down and allow them access.

Clarissa turned about, taking in her surroundings. This would once have been the hub of the house. A large kitchen table, solid and worn with age, still graced the centre of the room. Hand-carved wooden cabinets had been fitted around the walls, but now the doors were hanging off or completely missing and the contents had been ransacked. Drawers had been pulled open and their contents discarded all over the floor. Clarissa couldn't walk far without kicking something.

"What happened here?" asked Clarissa. "It looks like the house was hit by an earthquake."

The cat jumped up to the kitchen table and settled herself down in what must have been her customary spot. The light poured in through the window here and created a pool of warmth for her old bones.

"Local youths, mainly. Out for a spot of mischief. In her younger years, Mabel would have ensured they found it, for sure."

Toby pounced on her words. "She's still alive then?"

"I didn't say that." The cat waggled her head and primly tucked her paws under her body.

"But you insinuated that."

Toby relayed the cat's information to Clarissa, who had begun to search through the items on the floor for a tin opener. She started to fill the slots in the cutlery drawer with knives, forks and spoons and gathered up the larger cutlery items into a pile that she placed carefully on the draining board.

Clarissa, inclined to agree with Toby that the cat had given more away than she might have wished, straightened up, an old-fashioned tin opener in her hand.

"Is Mabel safe? Why don't you tell us where she

is?" she asked the cat, who turned her head away and stared at the back door.

Clarissa shrugged and stabbed at the can of tuna with the opener. "How does this thing work?" she grumbled. "Who even uses this kind of thing anymore?"

"Mabel does obviously," Toby suggested, ever helpful.

"Oh come on. You don't seriously think she's still living here, do you? Surrounded by this mess?"

Toby lifted his head and sniffed the air. "It's a great disguise. Off-putting for anyone that might imagine they'd find her here."

"If they came casually looking for her, you mean?" Clarissa had managed to open half the can. "You're right." She regarded the jagged edge of the lid with suspicion. She might be able to scoop the contents out, but she wasn't sure she could do so without losing a digit in the process.

In the end she decided nothing ventured, nothing gained, and opted to tease out the tuna with a teaspoon.

"You know if you'd bought a more expensive can of tuna it would have had a pull-top lid," Toby remarked. "They have all mod-cons in the supermarkets these days."

"I know that, Einstein. But I went for quantity rather than quality, and the cheaper ones come without any fancy accoutrements." She had finally filled a bowl. The cat continued to look studiously away from her, but her whiskers twitched.

Clarissa held the bowl out towards the cat's proud back. "Look," she said. "I'm not going to blackmail you. You look like a cat in need of a good dinner or three to me. You can have this regardless. And before we go, I'll leave the other cans out for you, but we would dearly love to talk to Mabel and make sure she's safe. There are bad people—"

"She knows all about bad people," the cat hissed, and now she looked straight at Clarissa. "We've met more of them than you've had hot dinners." Her head dropped so she could glare at Toby sitting on the floor below the table. "You turn up here with your fancy words and fake admonishments, but Mabel could turn the pair of you into cockroaches even on a bad day. Her magick is greater than your human's will ever be."

"What did she say?" asked Clarissa. "Will she tell us where Mabel is?"

"She says you'll be a great witch one day. We're just getting to Mabel's whereabouts," Toby lied smoothly.

The cat snorted. "You are a loyal familiar."

"I'm not her familiar. We're just friends. I was Old Joe's dog first and foremost. Although to be fair I had no idea he was a witch."

"Your third eye was opened." The cat nodded. "I can see it."

"For better or worse," Toby shrugged. "I'm not entirely sure yet."

"You have great power within you. Never doubt that. It is growing all the time. You have an interesting aura around you."

"Thank you," said Toby.

"But make no mistake, you are as much her familiar as she is your witch. Some things are meant to be."

Clarissa placed the bowl of tuna on the table in front of the cat. "Any joy?" she asked Toby.

"Such impatience." The cat sniffed the tuna.

"It smells good, doesn't it?" Toby licked his lips. "I promise you we only want to ask Mabel a few questions."

The cat sighed, closed her eyes and dipped her head. For a second Toby imagined she had fallen asleep but when she opened her eyes again, they shone with renewed life. "Go back into the garden and head down the bank towards the sea. Watch your step."

"Thank you!" Toby wagged his tail and glanced

back at Clarissa, who beamed. "We'll be back to open the other cans."

"Oh, don't worry about that." The cat sat up and twitched her whiskers. Toby heard the sound of metal against metal, and the lids from the two remaining cans of tuna that Clarissa had set on the work surface near the sink flew off and clattered to the floor. "Some things I can do myself."

Chapter Ten

"Did you see what she did?" Toby still couldn't believe it. They were winding their way down some steep steps, the grass and brambles towering above Toby and almost tickling Clarissa's chin. "I didn't know animals could do magic too."

"Will you watch where you're going?" Clarissa had her heart in her mouth. There was no railing here to catch a hold of, and Toby kept looking back. Either he'd miss his step and take a nasty fall, or she'd end up tripping over him.

"Did you know that?" Toby persisted. He had the sure-footed balance of a mountain goat, never putting a foot wrong.

"Yes," Clarissa replied, widening her eyes as the path twisted to the left and gave them a view of the beach about sixty feet below them. "Oh my word. This is giving me vertigo."

"You'd be no good on a broomstick," Toby tittered, and scampered down another dozen steps.

Once the path had flattened out a little, Clarissa paused for a rest and rubbed her chest. "I think I'm having a heart attack. What if we make it all the way down and she's not there?"

"I suppose we'll just have to come all the way back up again," replied Toby, doubling back to sit in front of her, his mouth open and his tongue lolling. "But I don't think we'll find her on the beach. I told you, she lives in a hedge."

Clarissa rolled her eyes. "I think you've got your terms wrong. There *is* such a thing as a hedge witch, but…"

She pulled up short.

An old woman had appeared out of nowhere on the path in front of them. Not more than five feet in height, she looked smaller than that, thanks to the hunch of her shoulders. Dressed in a flowing dark green dress and matching tunic, wrought from home-dyed rough hessian, she had some kind of utility belt slung around her hips that clanged and jittered when she walked. She had adopted a complicated headdress of braided bracken and twisted fern, interspersed with sprigs of cow parsley, and this sat low on her brow, juxtaposed prettily against her silvery hair. Her face, streaked in varying shades of green, had an ancient leathery quality, and her pale green eyes shone with brilliant intelligence.

"Well met." She stomped a long wooden staff on the ground and smiled. Half of her teeth appeared to be missing, the rest were crooked.

Clarissa peered down at Toby.

"Told you," he said.

Clarissa fought to cover her confusion. This woman, if indeed she were Mabel, appeared far older than she might have expected. Surely she would be a similar age to Miranda Dervish?

The woman cackled. A high-pitched sound that might have led you to question someone's sanity, had you not already been confronted by the oddest-looking woman in the south-west of England.

In Clarissa's experience anyway.

"Good afternoon." Clarissa stepped forward. "We were looking for Mabel Armistead?"

"Looks like you might have found her then." The woman cackled again.

Clarissa remained unconvinced. "I apologise for disturbing you—"

"'Tis no disturbance. Merrybutton told me you were on your way."

"Merrybutton? Is that the name of your cat?" Clarissa asked.

"'Tis the name I gave her. Not sure it's the name she would take for herself. But what's done is done. We've taken a few turns round the sun together, have Merrybutton and I."

"She's a... an erm... a beautiful cat."

"She's a feisty little madam, if the truth be told, but I has a sneaking kindly fondness for her." Mabel's eyes regarded them with some cunning. "Who be you then?"

Clarissa stepped forward. "I'm Clarissa Page and this is Toby."

Toby, displaying no signs of anxiety or fear, walked up to the old woman to stand in front of her. He wagged the tip of his tail. She leaned down and took his face in her free hand, looking deeply into his eyes. She smiled at what she saw there.

"You be a good boy," she told him. "And you're doing well, I think. You must continue to learn and grow. Merrybutton could help you with that, if she so wished."

She stood upright once more and shuffled forwards to get a closer look at Clarissa. She stared hard into the young woman's face, taking in every shadow and pore, the cut of her cheekbones and the thrust of her chin.

"Well, well... I must be getting old. I remember your father David as just a young lad, and yet here you are, full grown it seems."

"You knew my father?" Clarissa cocked her head in interest. Very few people had ever spoken to her about her parents. Her insides performed a strange loop to hear his name. She longed to know more.

"I did. I knew Old Joe better, of course." Mabel smiled softly, and Clarissa spotted a certain wistfulness in her expression. "He were a good man, that Joseph. A sad loss to us all."

"That's why we're here," Toby said. "We need to talk to you about the woman who killed him."

Mabel laughed in delight. "Why, you have a voice! How perfectly delicious. Did Old Joe do that?"

"No. Miranda Dervish did it."

This seemed to stop the old woman in her tracks. She leaned heavily against her staff. "Miranda did it, you say?"

"When she killed Old Joe." Toby sat by Mabel's feet and gazed up at her.

The old witch wheezed heavily, her eyes darkening. Her sunshine had been extinguished, and now her face had fallen and grown pale. "She did it, did she? What's she up to? I don't like to hear of her. It sends a cloud over the sun hearing that name. After all these years?" She spoke in a hushed voice, not really addressing Toby and Clarissa. She looked out to sea for some time, wavering against her stick, until finally, she turned about. "Follow me," she told them. "We probably need to have a little chat."

She led them through a narrow gap in the thick hedgerow that grew alongside the steep path. If you hadn't known to look for the entrance, you would never have spotted it there. The assumption of any casual walker would be that the hedge grew up the rocky cliff face, but actually this was an illusion, and the hedge transpired to be a dense but hollow pocket of greenery. Toby didn't have a problem following Mabel as she expertly turned and twisted her body to manoeuvre through the minute entrance, but Clarissa struggled, her hair and clothes snarling up against greedy burs and briars.

The thin corridor opened out into a wider area backing onto a shallow cave in the rockface. An iron kettle steamed over an open bonfire, and several tree stumps had been employed here as seats. The scattering of possessions around about and a small bed in the cave gave Clarissa and Toby the impression that Mabel had been living here for a while.

"When was the last time you ate?" Clarissa peered around, searching for anything edible.

"I don't need much," Mabel shrugged. "Merrybutton keeps me in the odd mouse."

Toby shuddered. "You eat mice?" Recalling the famished cat they'd left behind at the cottage, Toby could only assume that Merrybutton hadn't made much of a success of hunting of late. "Ewww. Clarissa bought her some tuna."

"I've a couple of sandwiches here I'm happy to share." Clarissa held up her bag. "Or failing that I can go and get something for you. Something decent." She didn't really fancy running up the hill again, but she could hardly leave Mabel without food.

"You're a good girl, you are. Kind. Just like your grandfather." She dropped her staff next to one of the tree stumps and indicated Clarissa should sit, then pottered around next to the fire. "I'll make us some tea. If all else fails, there's always tea."

"Why do hoomans always say that?" Toby asked, following Mabel as she made her way into the cave and rooted around for a canister of tea.

She found it and shook it, then lifted the lid and

peered inside. Satisfied, she hooked a teaspoon out of her belt and made her way back to the fire. "Probably because it's true, young man. What's your name again?"

"Toby," Toby reminded her.

"That's right. That's right."

She hummed as she prepared the teapot, turning inward. Toby eavesdropped as she chuntered to herself. "He seems like a decent enough fellow. Lots of potential, I'd say." She cocked her head, listening for a second, before cackling loudly. "Merrybutton, you be a bad cat. A naughty cat." She didn't sound disapproving, however.

Imagining Mabel had forgotten he and Clarissa were present, Toby whined.

The old witch came back to the present. "Merrybutton seems quite taken with you for some reason. I trust her judgement."

"Is Merrybutton alright?" Clarissa asked. "Only she seemed awfully thin."

Mabel frowned, and Clarissa grimaced inwardly, hoping the old witch hadn't taken what she'd said the wrong way. "I mean—"

"Oh, it's true." Mabel waved away any hint of apology. "I know you mean well. The thing is, Mad Mabel is getting a bit forgetful in her dotage. I can manage to get about. And I can climb the steps back to the house, but these days I'm less inclined to do so. I like it here." She gestured about at her humble surroundings. Above them, the dense foliage let in light, and yet at the same time the ground around them was relatively dry. "I like to feel the elements in my face. The saltiness of the sea on the wind. The gold blessings of the sun and the cool blessings of the moon's rays, they're all the same to me. Gifts from Gaia."

Clarissa nodded her understanding but couldn't imagine what it must be like to be out here in all weathers, especially in the winter. She liked her home comforts, did Clarissa.

Mabel must have read her mind. "It gets a bit parky at times." She fumbled with the nearest tree stump and to Toby's surprise, unlatched a small hidden door. It opened to disclose a pile of plates, glasses and mugs. Mabel extracted a pair of mismatched chipped china cups and a bowl. "No milk, I'm afraid." She grunted. "But if I did have some, old Merrybutton would be down here demanding it all, anyhow. I wouldn't see the going of it."

"She did seem hungry." Toby inspected the teapot. The heat from the spout warmed his nose.

"I can take a hint, young man. You think I'm neglecting my cat." She closed her eyes momentarily and smiled. "She still loves me, she do. Though she thinks I'm a pain in her nether regions."

Mabel poured the tea into the cups and half-filled the bowl. She handed Clarissa a cup and pushed the bowl under Toby's nose. He eyed it in distaste. "Get it down you, you fusspot," Mabel ordered him, and he tentatively stretched out his tongue before retreating in alarm.

"Well wait till it's cooled down, silly boy!" Mabel hooted her mirth, startling a couple of starlings nesting close by. She waved them away as they tweeted an angry protest her way. "You've not got the sense you was born with, my love."

The starlings settled back down on a branch close by, twittering like crazy. "Never mind my neighbours." She took a seat on a stump opposite Clarissa. "Never mind them at all. They're noisy beggars." She regarded Clarissa with an air of expectancy, and Clarissa, remembering her manners, sipped at her tea. It tasted good, refreshing and light, similar to green tea but with something a little dusky.

"My own blend," Mabel told her. "Nettle and lavender. 'Tis one of my favourites, too."

"It's lovely! Just what I needed." Clarissa fanned herself with her free hand. "I almost wish the weather would break and we'd have some rain."

Mabel tilted her head to stare up at what little sky they could see under the canopy of leaves above. "Another few days I reckon. A good storm's a-comin'. Wednesday," she decided.

"I take it you don't have television down here then?" Toby looked about. "Or a radio?"

"All the entertainment anyone ever needs is either in here," Mabel tapped her head and pulled a face, "or out there." She gestured back the way they'd come to the path beyond.

She drained her cup and looked expectantly at Clarissa. "So, my girl. Let's get down to business, shall us?"

"Yes." Clarissa hadn't made as much headway with her tea. Mabel's mouth must have been coated in asbestos. "I have so many questions."

Mabel pointed at Toby. "I met this young man once before. When I visited Old Joe's house. I'd walked all the way there, and I walked all the way home. That be a fair distance."

Clarissa, astonished, made a small 'o' shape with her mouth. Eleven or so miles. "You needed money rather badly?"

"I did. Not for me, you understand. I gets by. Most of the time. But—" Mabel hesitated, "—I... let's just say, I had my reasons. They may or may not become clear during the course of the rest of this conversation."

She poured herself more tea from the pot. "I'm guessing you're here to talk to me about Miranda Dervish, so let's get started."

Toby settled at Mabel's feet, resting his head on her bare toes, listening as she told her story. She didn't object. Occasionally she reached down to stroke his head.

"I was in my final year at Ravenswood when Miranda joined. I'd had rather a fun time of it. I come from a long line of Devon witches and we've been well known around here for centuries. I was a confident young lady, keen to practise my magick at every opportunity and not really overly interested in reading, writing and 'rithmetic as it was at that time." She smiled, her face glowing at the memory of those days. "I had so many friends; we had hot chocolate parties during the winter, and in the autumn term I was known to smuggle a bottle of my mother's home-brewed damson wine along." Mabel giggled. "I think my mother watered them down on purpose because she knew I'd half-inch one and make a fool of myself with my friends. She didn't want me getting into trouble at school. She was a bright one, was my mother."

"Miranda was younger than you?" asked Clarissa.

"Oh yes. By about five years. I was just about to join my coven as a neophyte."

Clarissa made a quick calculation. "So you were seventeen, and Miranda—"

"—was twelve or thirteen. Yes. That would be about right."

"She made an impression on you?"

Mabel screwed her forehead up and nodded. Taking a deep breath, she said, "She did. As I said, I knew magick. Had a natural instinct for it. Something bred inside me and nurtured by my mother and grandmother. It wasn't something I ever had to work at."

Clarissa remembered the days of learning magick and other skills at Ravenswood. Nothing had come particularly naturally to her. Grace Catesby, as her housemistress, had often said this was because she'd spent her formative years with her parents, who had denounced magick. She experienced a pang of envy, recalling how the other girls in her year had outperformed her at every turn.

"So I was a natural. A bit lazy. A fun-loving youngster with her whole witchy future mapped out. Miranda was something else altogether."

Clarissa looked up from her tea. Something subtle had changed in Mabel's voice. Where before she'd been exchanging pleasantries, memories of a distant past, now her tone had thickened, as though her very words were strangling themselves in her throat.

"Ravenswood is a natural home for us middle ranking witches, those of us who come from families that can't be bothered or can't afford to send their offspring to the grander schools in London or beyond. So I've never understood what compelled Miranda's family to enrol her there."

"What do you mean?"

"I mean—" Mabel thrust her jaw out and exhaled sharply. "She was a cold, hard child. Entirely self-contained. And the magick she practised reflected that on every level."

"How so?" asked Clarissa.

In answer, Mabel threw her cup at a tree stump. It smashed into several large pieces and a number of smaller ones. Toby jumped at the sudden violence of her actions and retreated hurriedly towards the cave. Clarissa half stood in shock, but Mabel shook her head and Clarissa resumed her seat.

"My apologies." Mabel waved a hand and the

pieces of the cup lying scattered on the ground around the stump began to shift and bind themselves together once more. The china melted at its broken edges and re-moulded itself. When it had completed the process, Mabel hooked a finger its way and the cup flew towards her. She caught it easily, as accomplished as any cricket fielder.

She held the cup out towards Clarissa. "Take it," she instructed the younger woman. "Tell me what you see."

A test of some kind? Clarissa stood and stepped forward to better examine the cup in the old witch's hands. "You've fixed it. It will hold liquid," Clarissa confirmed.

"But?" Mabel prompted her.

"But I can see hairline cracks. Here and here. I can see where the cup has been smashed." Clarissa ran her finger around the rim. "And there are tiny chips out of it too."

Mabel nodded. She reached down for the teapot and filled her cup once more with the now cooling liquid. It held the tea without any problems. "Yes, it's damaged. I could throw it away."

"But it's functional. It still does the job it was created to do."

A flash of triumph sparked in Mabel's eye. She

raised the cup in a toast to Clarissa. "Precisely. You are a witch with the truest of hearts. Someone who appreciates the flaws in an object or an animal or another person and learns to cherish them. Flaws are what make us unique as individuals."

"And Miranda wasn't this way?"

"Never. Not at all. She only ever desired perfection. In herself, in other people, in her magick." Mabel glanced over at Toby, who had taken a few steps out of the safety of the cave. "Come, come, my lad. You are braver than that." She beckoned to him and he trotted obediently to sniff her hand.

"Good lad," she said. "Good lad. I expect she saw perfection in you. For you are perfectly defined, perfectly created and perfectly divine." She lifted her head and rolled back her shoulders, staring at the sky. "Divine," she breathed, her voice a whisper of love and devotion. Dropping her head, she winked at Toby. "In all the ways that word can be construed. And for that, we give thanks."

Clarissa regarded her furry friend doubtfully. A wonderful friend perhaps. Divine? Hmm. Maybe not.

Mabel moved the bowl she'd previously poured for Toby closer to him. "You should drink this. It will do you good."

Clarissa drained her tea. "What did Miranda do if

things weren't perfect? Did she throw a tantrum? Did she keep trying?"

"Goodness me, no." Mabel held out the teapot so that Clarissa could refill her cup. "She simply destroyed what she didn't like."

"I thought at first that it was good old-fashioned rivalry. Although given the difference in our ages, I found it odd." Mabel cast her mind back, remembering her days at Ravenswood once more. "On the surface she appeared friendly enough, but quite quickly other students in my circle began to notice some strange occurrences."

"Like what?" Clarissa leaned closer.

"Silly things, initially. If I checked a book out of the library, she would reserve it straight away and I'd have my lending time cut short and would have to return it. No big deal. I wasn't the world's keenest reader." Mabel lifted a poker and stirred the fire before throwing on another log. "Then my closest friend, Cassandra, had an unfortunate accident and fell down the stairs. It meant she was sent home to recuperate and she had to miss the end of our academic careers. Again, it wasn't life or death stuff by any means, but I had been so looking forward to sharing the trials and tribulations of our final exams with her, and going to the end of year party together."

"That's understandable. When you've been right through school with someone it marks a rite of passage. Do you think Miranda was to blame?"

"At the time I didn't. Subsequently, I did." Mabel frowned. "I had plenty of friends, but for me Cassandra was my confidante, my buddy."

Clarissa opened her mouth to ask something, but a sudden crash startled her. She twisted about to see Toby staring at the ground, wide-eyed.

"I didn't touch it. It wasn't me." The bowl he'd been drinking tea from had somehow smashed.

"Toby," Clarissa scolded. "Be more careful."

"I swear it wasn't me," Toby repeated.

Mabel jiggled her hands at them both, dismissing the incident, a half-smile playing around her lips. "Don't worry. I pick my crockery up in the charity shops in town. There's always plenty more of people's castaways to be found." She tittered to herself for a moment and Clarissa wasn't sure what she'd found amusing, but didn't press the old woman. Instead, she drew her attention back to Miranda Dervish.

"Anything else?" she asked.

"Oh plenty," Mabel nodded, "but to cut a long story short, I'd been hoping to win a prize for magick at the end of year ceremony. Do you remember The Conjurer's Cup?"

Clarissa nodded.

"Every one of my foremothers who had attended Ravenswood had managed to win that prize. It was expected of me—"

"Let me guess. Miranda won it?"

"Yes. But it was the way she won it that is the story here." Mabel pressed her lips together in disapproval. "Somehow she must have been stalking me. The library books were one thing. The resources I used for potions and magick, that was entirely something else. She knew almost as well as I did what magick I intended to perform, how and when, and she either beat me to it or she performed something far bigger, more powerful or more outrageous than what I could even have considered."

Clarissa rested her elbows on her knees and her chin in her hands, thinking about what Mabel had said. She wasn't sure it proved much. *Coincidence?*

Mabel clearly read the doubt in her face.

"I started to suspect sabotage when my friends noticed what was happening and drew it to my attention. So we organised a double bluff. I let it be known that for the final part of my magick exam I would perform a spell that would make a statue come to life and dance. I think I'd been watching a Sinbad film. They were popular when I was young." She snorted at the memory. "I chose Terpsichore. Do you remember her? She graced the Great Hall."

Clarissa nodded. The Great Hall at Ravenswood had been lined with statues and icons of goddesses from any number of religions. Terpsichore, a tall statue carved from alabaster, stood in the corner near a side door. She remembered it for its scars and chips, when most of the other statues in the hall had been lovingly cared for and remained pristine.

"Now, had I been able to do that it would have been quite a coup. But we're talking magick far beyond my capabilities."

Clarissa could only agree. "It would have been a sight worth seeing. So you bluffed her."

"I did. And lo and behold, when we all came down for breakfast on the morning of my final exam, there was Terpsichore in pieces on the floor. One of the professors put her together over the summer that year, apparently. It took her weeks."

"You can still see the joins," Clarissa told Mabel. "I'd often wondered what happened to her."

"Instead of that I borrowed a dolls' house from the younger students, and I transformed that into a living, breathing masterpiece." Mabel smiled at the memory. "A little boy on his rocking horse, Father reading the paper. Mother taking tea in the parlour and a little girl playing with her dolly. Even in the kitchen I had a tiny cook baking a minuscule apple pie, while in the attic a housemaid made the beds. Smoke came out of the chimney. Oh! It was an incredible sight! And such fun." Mabel leaned forward to whisper conspiratorially, "I can still smell that pie now."

"That sounds amazing," Clarissa agreed. "But you said you didn't win the prize?"

"One of the rules for the prize, if you recall, was that you had to repeat the magic in front of all those parents and dignitaries who graced the end-of-year Awards ceremony with their presence. I passed my exam with flying colours. Unfortunately, on the evening of the Awards ceremony, the dolls' house arranged in pride of place on a pedestal in front of the stage in The Great Hall, ready for me to demonstrate my prowess, burned down."

"Oh my word!" Clarissa clapped her hands to her mouth.

"In front of everybody." Mabel's eyes sparkled with unshed tears at the memory of it. She offered Clarissa a brittle smile. "And all the little dolls inside were incinerated."

Clarissa gasped. Clearly Mabel could still experience the pain of that moment. "And you think—?"

"That it was Miranda? Oh yes." Mabel nodded,

her voice emphatic. "She was overt about it. We were standing together in the wings, ready for the ceremony. She turned to me and said, 'I have something spectacular to show you.' And she poked her head out from the side of the curtains and with just a twitch of her finger, the house was ablaze. I ran out but it was too late. And it was peculiar, because the fire wasn't hot. It was ice-cold! But my beautiful house burned to ashes in literally less time than it takes to tell the story."

Clarissa regarded Mabel in horror. An icy fire? That had to be dark magick. "You must have explained what happened to the professors, though?"

"I tried, but they thought it was tittle-tattle, and as you know, that sort of thing wasn't encouraged. At least not while I was a student at Ravenswood. Perhaps it's changed now."

Clarissa wasn't sure it had really. Students were required to live on their wits most of the time. Excuses were never encouraged.

"And so Miranda was given the prize. One of many she won in her time at Ravenswood. I departed the institution for the final time the very next day, but not before this little upstart of a thirteen-year-old girl had pulled me to one side and told me to forget all I'd seen and never to conjecture. If I didn't, she'd track me down and 'do' for me." Mabel snorted.

Clarissa gasped. "Do for you? She said that?"

Mabel levelled clear eyes on Clarissa. "That's exactly what she said. She'd 'do' for me. And she tapped my head... just here." She gently touched the centre of her own forehead with the tip of her finger.

Toby had been following the discussion intently, and now he growled, then barked, once, twice. "That's how she killed Old Joe."

"It doesn't surprise me." Mabel's jaw clenched and her eyes grew hard. "She meant it. I know she did. I can still feel her finger on my forehead. I swear I felt a chill that day that all these years later has never really left me." She shivered, as though to emphasise her words. "I left Ravenswood and I tried to go out into the world to live my best life, to become the best me. The me my family expected me to be. As successful as my foremothers had been."

She shook her head. "But wherever I went, whatever I tried to do, something would happen. Something small, or unlucky, or odd, and I would feel..." Mabel took a deep breath, "...diminished somehow."

"Do you think Miranda was behind these things that happened?" Clarissa asked.

Mabel shrugged. "Who knows? Not I." She gave out her characteristic cackle, but Clarissa could hear how forced it sounded. "Some people would call these little unfortunate incidents fate. Bad luck. Life maybe. And they'd be right." She sucked her cheeks in. "Yes, yes. They'd be right, true enough."

"But you don't *really* believe that?" Clarissa reasoned if she did, she wouldn't be confiding in her.

The old woman shook her head violently, her headdress waving about. She sighed. "For many years I thought of myself as a failure. But old Mabel is no failure, and she's nobody's fool. Instead of trying to live in the wide world I retreated here, to Scavenger Cottage, and increasingly my circle has shrunk. I like it that way, just fine."

"But you've struggled for money." Clarissa understood now.

Mabel nodded. "Your grandfather understood. He knew all about Miranda. He was happy to help me."

"Then we will too!" Clarissa interjected, and Toby wagged his tail in emphatic agreement.

"Anything to get one over on The Pointy Woman," he said. "I hate her, I do."

"I've no doubt she'll feed off your hate," Mabel said. "It will suit her to do so. When I knew her there was an unmistakeable malevolence about Miranda. She wanted to be... not necessarily the best, but the most powerful. The one everyone talked about."

"And that's the odd thing, isn't it?" Clarissa sat up,

a sudden thought occurring to her. "I have tried to research into her, but it's really difficult to find anything out. People are unwilling to talk about her. Some even go so far as to claim they don't know her."

"Oh, they'll know her all right. Or know *of* her. And there will be material written about her, and photos taken, I'm certain. But someone, somewhere is covering up for her." Mabel looked troubled.

"Who?"

Mabel shrugged. "That's probably not the most important question."

"Well, *why* are they covering for her, then?" Clarissa asked, her brow furrowed.

Mabel spread her hands out. "The who and the why is something you're going to have to find out."

"We may have an inkling." Clarissa reached for her handbag and rummaged around in the pocket that might normally have held her mobile phone. She drew out the matchbox and, standing, came closer to the fire to show Mabel the contents.

"On the day that Old Joe was murdered, a purple gemstone was taken from his house. Toby witnessed the whole thing." The women glanced at Toby simultaneously, and he slowly twitched his tail, acknowledging the sadness of the memory of that day. "Then a few days ago, my neighbour—Old Joe's friend, a Mrs

Crouch—was attacked and left for dead. I found this in her house. She'd hidden it. I'm fairly sure Miranda was after this."

Clarissa pushed open the matchbox. The stone had been wrapped in tissue paper, but even so it shone with a bright blue light that cast a wondrous glow over everything within their vicinity. Clarissa unwrapped the tissue paper and Mabel blinked in surprise, leaning forward to examine the stone more closely, her fingers hovering above it as though sensing its energy.

"Glorious," Mabel said, her tone hushed.

Clarissa studied the older witch's face. "Do you have any idea what it is?"

Mabel shook her head, her lips pulled into a thin line. "None. You said Old Joe had one too?"

"A purple one. Except his was star-shaped."

Mabel cocked her head, thinking. "My deduction would be that they belong to a set or a collection." She shook her head slightly, and when she spoke again she sounded troubled. "Clarissa, if I were you I would take enormous care. If Miranda is hunting for these, they must be worth a great deal to her. And if that's the case, they're probably immensely powerful."

Clarissa wrapped the stone in its tissue once more, muting its bright light. She dropped her head and sighed, disappointed Mabel didn't know anything about them.

"And dangerous," Mabel added, and Clarissa met her eyes once more. "You must be careful."

"I will."

Mabel frowned. "I be worried. Truly. There has to be someone out there who knows what these stones are for. And maybe someone who can keep this one safe for you. If Miranda knew you had it—"

"I'm pretty sure she must know we have it," Clarissa said.

"Then all the more reason to find someone who can take it off your hands. What about the High Priestess of your coven?"

"Lady Amphitrite? No. She banished me from the coven for the foreseeable future after I started asking questions about Miranda Dervish. Miranda is a member of the Coven of the Silver Winds too."

"Of course. Of course." Mabel rolled her eyes. "I'd lost track… but yes." Mabel reached down to retrieve her staff and hauled herself upright. "That's an even more sinister situation. What you're talking about here is corruption at a very high level."

She gestured towards the exit to the clearing. It would take them out to the cliff path. Clearly, it was time for Clarissa to leave. "You have to take it higher. Perhaps to the Ministry of Witches."

"But how can I possibly know who to trust?" Clarissa asked. "In the past week I've lost both my job and my place in the coven. A few months ago, Miranda tried to have Toby put to sleep in a shelter." Realising Toby wasn't following them, the women turned around.

The dog had his back to them, his bushy tail wagging like a helicopter blade.

"Go home and put that stone somewhere safe," Mabel told Clarissa. "As for finding someone you can trust, leave that with me. I have some good contacts. There aren't many of our kind I don't know. Let me see if I can find you a name who can help you out."

"Thanks. I appreciate it." Clarissa placed her hand on the other woman's arm. It felt good to finally have a friend.

"Come on Toby. We need to get back," Clarissa called, and Toby moved aside so that she could finally see what he'd been doing. Clarissa's eyes widened.

The broken bowl he'd been drinking tea from had been fixed. The scars were apparent, the edges were ragged, and there were several chips around the rim... and yet, if he could have managed the teapot, he could have refilled the bowl and taken a drink from his bowl once more.

"You did *not* do that," Clarissa gasped, and turned to Mabel, expecting the old witch to confess that she'd actually fixed the bowl.

Mabel shook her head and smiled. "Not me."

"I did it!" Toby announced, his tail high, his eyes gleaming. "I watched Mad Mabel fix her cup, and I did the same!"

"But how?" Clarissa retraced her steps and bent down to examine the bowl.

"I thought it and I made it happen."

Mabel tittered and slammed her staff on the ground so hard, several dozen starlings erupted from the canopy and flew about her head, twittering in alarm. "I told you, my pet. That little lad is divine."

CHAPTER ELEVEN

Clarissa had spent most of the evening researching a story to send to *Witches Weekly* on the off-chance they'd look favourably on her work and buy it to include in a future edition. So far, she'd written:

Winifred Breezeazy came from the wrong side of the sticks. A freak childhood accident left her blind in one eye, and her parents reiterated over and over she would amount to nothing. Yet this little girl, with her shabby clothing and eyepatch, who ran barefoot around the narrow lanes of Tumble Town, and ran errands for the shady characters who conducted their business inside the pubs and inns there, went on to become one of the Ministry of Witches' best-loved and notorious councillors.

Clarissa read back what she'd written, deleted a sentence and started again, then stopped to think, her hands poised above her keyboard. Would this grab the reader enough?

Her concentration was abruptly interrupted by the sound of yet another mug breaking. Clarissa rolled her eyes and scraped her chair back.

"You know, we won't have anything decent to drink our tea out of at this rate," she called through to the kitchen.

"I'm fixing things!" Toby's exuberant response drew her towards the kitchen. An old bone-china cup with a pink-flowered rim dangled in the air in front of his face, ready to be dropped onto the floor.

"Whoa whoa whoa!" Clarissa reached out and grabbed the pretty cup. It formed part of an already incomplete set Clarissa had found in a kitchen cupboard. Clarissa imagined it must once have belonged to her grandmother, Old Joe's wife. Clarissa knew even less about Old Joe's wife than she did about him. While clearing and cleaning the house, Clarissa had started to fantasise about the objects she found, and created stories to explain Old Joe's life. The tea set —she had decided—had been a wedding gift from his bride's favourite aunt. Clarissa had imagined Old Joe had probably not appreciated the tea set to begin with–too pink and flowery and pretty-pretty–but after his wife's death he'd recognised it as one of her treasures and continued to use it to honour his late wife's memory.

Whatever the story, Clarissa didn't want the tea service smashed into pieces and then reset—probably incredibly badly—by a dog intent on practising his newly-found skills.

"Awww! You're a complete spoilsport. How else can I improve?" Toby complained. "Mabel said I needed to keep on experimenting."

"I'll buy you a cheap batch of worthless crockery from a charity shop in the morning, if you insist. I do think that Mabel was suggesting you try some other pieces of magick, not just keep smashing up the kitchen for the rest of your life."

"You sound a little grumpy, Clarissa," Toby wiggled his eyebrows at her. "Do you need a nap?"

Clarissa snorted. "You... are an impudent little horror. What I *need* is to be able to get on with my work, uninterrupted by crockery Armageddon out here."

"I think you're exaggerating," said Toby, but he backed away from the crockery cupboard and checked out his food bowl instead.

"Maybe you could move on to something a little more complicated? How about learning how to open cans of dog food?" Clarissa suggested.

"Like Merrybutton did with the tuna?" Toby nodded. "That's a great idea."

Clarissa opened the larder to locate one of his favourites. "Here we are. Beef stew with carrots and kale. Yummy. Why don't you have a go at this?"

Toby's eyes began to shine. "If I open the can, may I eat all of it?"

Clarissa laughed. There was no pull-top on this can. It had to be opened using a tin opener. Even she wouldn't be able to pull off this feat of magick.

"Of course."

Several hours later, Clarissa was finally happy with the copy she'd produced, and the article on Winifred Breazeazy's interesting childhood had come to life. Given the lateness of the hour, she decided she would check it over once more in the morning before sending it off with a covering email.

She leaned backwards in her chair, rolling her shoulders, stretching her diaphragm and breathing deeply. She'd intended to call the hospital again to check on Mrs Crouch but, glancing at the time on the screen, Clarissa decided it was probably a little late for that. She yawned and rubbed at her eyes.

Maybe she'd make herself a cup of Chamomile tea and take Toby for his late-night stroll around the block.

Toby.

What could he be up to?

Clarissa turned her head to one side. He'd been very quiet since the crockery stand-off.

She quietly pushed her chair back and tilted her head to listen.

Nothing.

Frowning, she made her way through to the dark kitchen, until she could hear a rapid lapping sound coupled with some snuffly nose-breathing.

"Toby?" Clarissa asked the darkness and fumbled against the wall for the light switch. As she bathed the room in a bright yellow glow, Toby, lying spread-eagled on the floor in classic 'frog' pose, blinked up at her in surprise. He had gravy all over the top of his snout and whiskers.

He'd actually managed to open the tin of dog food.

"I'm finding it hard to reach the very bottom of the can," he explained.

Clarissa's jaw dropped. "I don't believe you," she said. "How?"

"If I can think it, I can do it," Toby explained. "I've told you. It took me a while though. At least fifty or sixty attempts." He yawned. "I'm really tired now. All this magick takes it out of you, doesn't it?"

Clarissa reached down and examined the tin, afraid that left unsupervised he'd end up cutting himself to ribbons, but he'd managed to neatly excise the lid around the inside of the top, where the tin was thicker. Some traces of gravy remained among the bottom ridges of the can, but apart from that, the metal shone where he'd licked it clean.

"You amaze me," Clarissa said. "Come on, David Copperfield. Let's take a quick promenade around the block so you can wave at your many admirers, and then we'll head for beddy-byes."

They pootled slowly around the block, stopping for sniffs and wees—for Toby, not Clarissa obviously. For her part, Clarissa enjoyed the scent of the various flowers whose fragrance seemed stronger at night than during the day, and she lingered in places, in no rush to head home. Finally, however, their front door came into view.

A huge fluffy cat, mostly white but with striking black and orange markings around its face, sat on their front doorstep, licking its front paw at leisure.

Clarissa grabbed a hold of Toby's collar, assuming he would chase the cat away, but Toby, full of beef stew and carrots, and content after their little meander around the neighbourhood, was inclined not to bother.

"Greetingsssss," the cat purred.

"Good evening." Toby wagged his tail. He had started to warm to the idea of cats. The two he'd met today seemed particularly friendly.

"My name is Boogaloo. I have a messsssage for you."

Toby looked up at Clarissa. "He says his name is Boogaloo and he has a message for us."

"Boogaloo?" she repeated. "That's such a cute name." She dropped Toby's lead and stepped towards the cat to pet him. Boogaloo cast a wary eye at the dropped end of the lead but gave in to Clarissa's ministrations. "Who's the message from?"

Boogaloo, deciding enough was enough with the petting, dodged out of Clarissa's grasp. "Merrybutton. Over Beer way apparently. Sssshe ssssent the messssage via Catvine."

"Catvine?" Toby queried. "Is that like Twilight Barking?"

"The ssssame ssssort of prinsssciple," Boogaloo agreed. "But we're not limited to a ssssspecific time of the day." His smooth response rather suggested to

Toby that Boogaloo considered cats to be eminently superior with regard to their ability to communicate across distances, *whenever* they chose.

Toby decided to gloss over this for the time being. "What's the message?"

"You should sssseek out a booksssseller in Abbottssss Cromleigh," Boogaloo recounted.

"Abbotts Cromleigh?" Toby glanced up at Clarissa.

"That's a little town inland of here." She raised her eyebrows. "What about it?"

"He says we need to find a bookseller there."

"Any idea of the bookseller's name? You know, in case there's more than one bookshop. It's only a small town so I assume there won't be, but all the same—"

The cat stood and stretched, arching his back. He swaggered down the steps to rub his face against Toby's, before squinting up at Clarissa. "Hisss name is Misssssster Kephissssto," he said.

Clarissa had to push hard against the bookshop's door to gain entrance. It appeared to stick, but when she tried a little more force it swung open readily enough, and the old-fashioned bell jingled to notify the owner of her arrival.

The Storykeeper bookshop resided in an old Elizabethan building that resembled the prow of a ship, its black and white frontage arching into the narrow street outside. The windows on the floors above were paned with old diamond-shaped glass, although the shop windows themselves appeared more recent—recent in that they were Victorian rather than sixteenth-century, that is. The building was one of several in a row that spoke of Abbotts Cromleigh's history. Forty years ago, this row of ancient shops had been deemed an eyesore and the council had considered razing them to the ground and replacing them with something more modern, but nothing had happened. Over time the structures had been sold on and gentrified, and now they had all achieved protected status.

Clarissa knew all this because she had spent an hour on Google this morning searching for bookshops in the town, and for information about a Mr Kephisto. She'd found little in the way of information about the bookseller, but the research had confirmed that The Storykeeper was indeed the only shop selling books in town.

She wandered inside, staring round at the

higgledy-piggledy shelving that meandered off to the rear of the shop where the uneven roof dropped lower. The interior of this building would have made a great place to play hide and seek. Clarissa had clipped Toby to his lead, and now he sniffed at the foot of some shelving. *'Bestsellers'*, announced the sign on top of the display. Clarissa, a keen reader, reached out to touch the velvety gloss of one of the covers. She itched to take some of the books down and flick through their pristine pages, but without a job and an income, she needed to keep her spending to a minimum. It would be far better for her bank balance to resist all temptation while here.

Besides, she was on a mission.

"Hello?" she called, when no-one immediately appeared to greet her.

"Kephisto! Kephisto!" An unnatural squawking startled Clarissa, and she tilted her head up to search for the source of the noise. There appeared to be a mezzanine level above them. A crow, on a perch, gazed down at them with bright, intelligent eyes.

"Hi!" Clarissa said. "You're a handsome chap. What do you reckon, Toby?"

Toby gazed up at the crow with a certain amount of trepidation. He'd heard tales of birds divebombing dogs on occasion, and as he'd actually never seen a bird inside a building before, he considered this an unknown and potentially life-threatening situation. "Very handsome." He fixed the bird with a do-not-even-think-of-messing-with-me look and returned to his sniffing.

"Is Mr Kephisto around?" Clarissa asked the crow, not so much with the idea that the bookseller and the crow communicated, but more on the off-chance someone else might hear her and come to her aid.

"Kephisto! Kephisto!" the bird squawked again, and Clarissa heard the sound of a door closing, followed by light footsteps tripping down the stairs ahead of her.

"Kephisto! Kephisto!"

"I hear you, Caius," a gentleman answered. Clarissa peered around a particularly tall shelving display and finally spotted a slight man with a neatly trimmed beard and moustache. Of a decent vintage, Clarissa immediately identified him as a wizard, despite his civilian clothing. Smartly dressed in a light-coloured three-piece suit, with a pale blue cravat, here was a man who oozed ancient magick and formidable knowledge.

"Good afternoon, Madam." He peered over the top of his round spectacles at her. "How may I be of assistance? Are you looking for something in particular?"

Clarissa had tried to rehearse what she would say, but now she found that words failed her. She opened her mouth and closed it again. Where should she begin?

"It's not *something* we're looking for, it's *someone*," Toby butted in, deciding to take the lead. "Boogaloo told us to come here and speak to Mr Kephisto."

"Well, you've found me." Mr Kephisto didn't appear phased at all that Toby could talk to him. "But Boogaloo?" He shook his head, seemingly nonplussed.

"He's one of the cats in our neighbourhood. We live in Durscombe, in Sun Valley," Toby explained.

"Ah, I see." Mr Kephisto beamed down at the dog. "A knowledgeable chap, this Boogaloo, is he?"

"Apparently he was sent the message through the Catvine, via Merrybutton." Toby wagged his tail.

"Ah! Merrybutton! Her, I know well. How is she?"

"Old," said Toby. "And a bit feisty."

Mr Kephisto roared with laughter. "'Twas ever thus. And Mabel?"

"Bonkers."

Clarissa gasped. "Toby! I told you—"

Mr Kephisto, still chuckling, waved a hand at Clarissa. "Don't worry. Mabel would be the first to admit she's not what most mortals would consider normal. But abnormal is nothing to be ashamed of. It's just something that's a little bit different to what society expects."

Clarissa nodded. "True." She stuck out her hand. "I'm Clarissa Page, and this is Toby."

Mr Kephisto shook her hand. His skin, when he grasped hers, was dry and papery and cool to the touch. Clarissa wondered how old he was.

"Clarissa Page, the journalist on the *Sun Valley Tribune*?"

Clarissa's eyes lit up. She rarely had any professional recognition, so when someone recognised her name, it gave her a buzz. "Yes. Well, I was. They let me go."

"Really?" Mr Kephisto frowned. "I'm sorry to hear that. I read all of the local East Devon papers and I have to say, I very much enjoyed your writing. Especially the information piece on the kennels. Some good research went into that article."

"Thank you. Yes, it was a topic close to home."

"You should write more of that kind of thing."

"I certainly hope to do more investigative journalism in the future," Clarissa agreed. "In the meantime, I'm trying my hand at freelance work. Sending articles and stories off to… specialist magazines and journals."

"Very wise." Mr Kephisto tapped his nose. "I'm sure that's a strategy that will pay off for you."

He gestured to the rear of the shop. "Where are my manners? Can I interest you in some tea?"

Clarissa glanced around. Nobody else appeared to be in the shop. "I would hate to drag you away from your work."

"Oh, you won't be, I promise." Mr Kephisto made a small motion with the fingers on his right hand, and the front door locked behind them. "Besides, this is part and parcel of my work." He pointed towards the stairs. "Shall we?"

Clarissa settled onto one of the two comfortable high-backed chairs on the mezzanine level. Toby, rolling his eyes at Caius, settled at her feet. On the table between the chairs sat a tray with a teapot covered in a hand-knitted cosy, two cups on saucers, a milk jug and a sugar bowl, and a plate of assorted biscuits. Either Mr Kephisto had expected company, or he'd magicked these up while they chatted downstairs.

Mr Kephisto took the chair opposite Clarissa and steepled his fingers, evidently waiting for her to talk.

"My full name is Clarissa Louise Page Silverwind," she began, and Mr Kephisto nodded as though he'd known this all along.

"You're Joseph Silverwind's granddaughter," he said.

"Yes." Clarissa reached down and stroked Toby's head. "And this is Toby. He was Joseph's dog."

"And a very good boy, I've heard." Mr Kephisto reached into his jacket pocket and pulled out a dog treat. "May I?" he asked Clarissa, but he didn't wait for permission, simply leaned over and gave it to the dog.

"Thank you," Toby said, and devoured it in one chomp.

"I was sorry to hear about Joseph. I knew him from way back. He was a gentle man and a gentleman. He didn't deserve what happened to him."

Clarissa nodded her appreciation for his words. "Toby was there on the afternoon Joseph was killed."

"So he saw who killed Joseph?" Mr Kephisto regarded Toby with interest.

"Not only did he see the woman who murdered my grandfather, she bewitched him too."

"He can communicate with witches and wizards? I noticed that. It's a clever spell."

"There's more. Recently he's started to perform magick. Simple stuff, but his rate of improvement is astronomical. It took me years to learn some of what he can do. And now he can also identify the subjects of photographs. I have a sneaking suspicion he's starting to make out written words too."

"He's learning to read?"

"Yes. I believe so."

Toby stared up at them both with innocent eyes, blinking once and hoping he looked suitably modest. Then he ruined it all. "I got skillz."

Clarissa tutted and sighed, but she couldn't hide her amusement.

"If that's true—and I don't doubt your word--you'll have to work with him to make sure he knows how to control any magick he uses. It could be—"

"Disastrous?" Clarissa suggested, raising her eyebrows in amusement.

Mr Kephisto snorted. "I was thinking more… ah… interesting, rather than disastrous."

"Don't worry. I'll keep an eye on him."

"But that's not why you're here?" Mr Kephisto lifted the teapot and began to pour the rich ruby-gold liquid into the cups.

"No." Clarissa lifted her handbag onto her lap. "I have something to show you, but first let me fill you in on the story so far."

"How is Mrs Crouch doing?" Mr Kephisto frowned over the dregs of his tea. All of the biscuits had long since disappeared but the teapot never seemed to empty.

"She's still the same. Stable but critical, the hospital say. She hasn't woken up at all since the night I found her. The doctors are worried she might have brain damage."

"Curious." Mr Kephisto leaned back in his chair and stared at the ceiling. He remained quiet for a minute or two while Clarissa watched him. Eventually he dropped his gaze to her once more. "I vaguely know Ivy Crouch. Very vaguely." He scratched his forehead. "I can't remember why. To be honest, she has been flying under my radar. I can only imagine, in light of what you've been telling me, that this is intentional. Given that she's never been fully active in the community... and that you yourself didn't know she was a witch... I'm sat here considering whether she's a sleeper or not."

"A sleeper?" Clarissa had no idea what Mr Kephisto was referring to.

"Yes." He placed his cup on top of his saucer. "An agent working for—I would imagine in her case—the Ministry of Witches."

Clarissa gaped at Mr Kephisto. "An agent? Like James Bond you mean?"

Mr Kephisto chuckled. "That kind of thing, yes."

"But she's… old." Clarissa screwed her face up. "I mean, not Old Joe kind of old, but getting there. Sixties maybe."

"Ah, the disdain of youth," sighed Mr Kephisto. "Sixty is not old, my dear."

"It's just—" Clarissa, aware that Mr Kephisto might be far older than that, tried to backpedal, "I thought agents were young, ninja-like creatures? You know? Fearless, ex-special forces. And male?"

"If every agent fit that description our enemies would know exactly who to look out for, wouldn't they?"

"Clever Kephisto! Clever Kephisto!" the crow squawked, startling Toby, who shot to his feet assuming Bird War Three was about to be unleashed.

"Shh Caius!" Mr Kephisto remonstrated with it, and it ceased its clamouring.

"Hmm," said Clarissa in the ensuing silence, sitting back in her seat. No matter how she conjured up the image, she couldn't quite get her head around the absurd notion that Mrs Crouch might be a special agent for the Ministry of Witches.

"I have a hunch," Mr Kephisto announced. "Mrs Crouch is in which hospital?"

"Wonford. In Exeter."

"Alright. I may go and visit her."

"I've tried. They won't let me see her because I'm not close family."

"Mundane rules and regulations," Mr Kephisto sniffed. "There are ways to work around these things." He drummed his fingers together, considering Clarissa's story once more. "Which brings me to Miranda Dervish."

Toby, who had lain back down on Clarissa's feet, growled.

"I quite understand, young man," Mr Kephisto told him. "Fortunately, Ms Dervish is far from an unknown quantity, unlike poor Mrs Crouch."

"You know of her then?" asked Toby.

"Oh yes. Her reputation precedes her wherever she goes. My most recent intelligence on the matter was that she'd worn out her welcome and been forced abroad. Italy or somewhere. I wonder what brought her home, and why she killed Joseph."

Clarissa offered the wizard a rueful smile. "I saved that information for last." She reached into her handbag and drew out the matchbox. "Whatever The

Pointy Woman was looking for inside Mrs Crouch's house, she failed to find it. I have it here."

Mr Kephisto's eyes widened in surprise. The blue gemstone lay on Clarissa's palm, casting its glorious light far and wide. He reached out, not to take it from her but to feel the energy it threw off. He breathed out heavily. "Incredible," he whispered.

"I told you that Miranda Dervish stole a gemstone from the carriage clock in Old Joe's living room. Well, it was remarkably similar to this one, except it was purple and star-shaped. Do you know what these are?"

Mr Kephisto slumped into stunned silence; his fist rammed against his mouth. Clarissa could almost hear the sound of the cogs whirring in his brain. Eventually he huffed. "I think I have an inkling." He jumped to his feet. "Follow me," he said.

Clarissa and Toby traipsed after him as he opened a door at the side of the mezzanine. "Keep watch, Caius," Mr Kephisto called back as he led the pair of them up the stairs.

"Caius! Caius!" Echoes of the crow's shrill calls followed them up the narrow staircase. At the top, Mr Kephisto unlocked another door and led them into the loft space. The wizard obviously lived and worked here when he wasn't in the shop.

The walls in this main room were lined with even more bookshelves, but these contained Mr Kephisto's private and personal collection. "This is an archive of all the records I've discovered relating to witchcraft in the south-west of England."

Clarissa spun round and round, entranced by the sheer quantity of material stored here. If she'd thought Temperance House had a decent archive, it paled into insignificance in comparison to what she could see here. "Incredible."

"I even have oral transcripts. In fact, some of my material predates the prevalence of the written word."

"Wow." Clarissa edged up closer to a group of shelves with black leather-bound volumes and perused the titles. "Do you think there's anything in these about the gemstones?"

"Not in those, but if I'm not mistaken—" Mr Kephisto retreated to the far reaches of the room, "—amongst these papers..." He pulled out a solid cardboard box and picked through the numerous slender folders it contained. "Oh, where is it?" he muttered. "I'm sure it was in conversation with a witch named Jebediah Hornbrook. Where is he?"

Toby scampered across the floor and nuzzled up

next to the wizard, peering into the box. "You should just let Clarissa drop the whole thing. That way the thing you're looking for will surface. It works every time for Clarissa." He peered over his shoulder at Clarissa, who was pursing her lips. "Doesn't it?"

"Not on purpose," Clarissa pointed out. "And we used a spell in Temperance House."

"It's a good idea, though." Mr Kephisto ran his hands over the top of the files. "Expose Jebediah!" he told the box, and the contents shifted. Nothing worked its way to the top, however.

Mr Kephisto turned to Toby. "Well, young man. What do you make of that?" His eyes twinkled at the dog. "It doesn't appear to have worked. Can you sense anything?"

Toby offered a little side-eye to Mr Kephisto. Something *had* happened. He'd detected a sudden warmth and a charge of energy, and he was sure the wizard must have felt it too. Could Mr Kephisto be indulging him? Toby let it pass and sniffed each and every file until something seemed to call to him. He poked his nose at it. "This one."

Mr Kephisto reached in and pulled out the file. "Very good. Very good indeed, Toby." He nodded to his desk. "Come," and they walked across together. Mr

Kephisto switched a lamp on. Clarissa joined them there.

"This is a transcript I made many years ago." He flipped open the folder and showed Clarissa a sheet of parchment. It contained a beautiful line drawing of a tree with handwritten text underneath. "Jebediah couldn't write, so I had him tell me his story and I wrote it down for future posterity."

"What language is this?" Clarissa asked, running her fingers over the beautifully written script.

"Old English. You'd probably recognise some of the words if you looked closely enough, but I can translate."

"Old English? But you said you took the transcript?" Clarissa wrinkled her brow.

"That's right." Mr Kephisto did not illuminate any further.

He angled the lamp over the page and peered at it more closely. "Right, yes. I remember. Jebediah lived in the forest, deep in the Blackdown Hills. He had very little to do with the population at large and preferred the company of the foxes, badgers and deer to any of the villagers thereabouts. For the most part, they all lived in harmony and nobody bothered him. He supplied them with wood and game, and they left him to his own devices. He lived to a grand old age."

"So what's this?" Clarissa tapped the image of the tree. An enormous beech tree by the look of it. The illustrator had taken care to sketch in the bark. Under the light of Kephisto's desk lamp, the tree seemed to float off the page. It looked incredibly realistic, albeit tiny at approximately six inches tall; Clarissa could almost feel the texture of it beneath her fingertips.

"None of us lives forever, and when his time was up, Jebediah—knowing he had no heirs—came to me to tell me about a tree in the centre of Bucklebeare Wood. This is an image of the tree as best as I could draw it."

"You did this? It's extraordinary."

"Thank you. Jebediah gave me a number of vivid descriptions of the tree and insisted on seeing each version of the image I drew. He made me change it several times. I believe this is as close as it was possible to get."

"You never saw the tree itself?"

"Goodness me, no. Jebediah took the secret of its location to the grave. I remember its general whereabouts, but that's it."

Clarissa studied the paper. "What's so special about it? Why do you think there's a link between the stones and this tree?"

Mr Kephisto peered over the top of his spectacles at Clarissa. "In the magickal realms that exist at the cusps of mundane society, nothing is ever as it appears." He gave the parchment a gentle shake. "Watch this."

Toby jumped up, resting his front paws against the edge of the table so that he too could see.

The parchment shimmered gently, the words pulsing fractionally until they seemed to lift off the page and scramble and unscramble in front of the eyes of the spectators. The branches of the tree started to shimmy gently as though disturbed by a soft breeze. They too lifted from the page, reaching into the air, all spindly fingers and trembling leaves. The tree began to grow out of the parchment, reaching, reaching. At first just an inch, then three inches and eight inches and outwards and upwards, growing taller and taller. Clarissa and Toby fell back in synchronised surprise, Toby opening his mouth to bark before forgetting his intention as the tree continued its upward trajectory. Taller it grew, taller and taller, until it finally stood several feet high, semi-translucent and yet full of energy and colour.

"Wow!" Clarissa stretched out tentative fingers. The tree wasn't solid, but something held her hand away. A protective force field, perhaps?

Toby ducked underneath the outlying branches, his ears twitching. "I see a squizzel on the tree!" Something darted along a branch and disappeared inside a small crevice in the trunk.

Clarissa squatted next to him and followed his line of vision. "I saw it too!" she confirmed, her voice rising with excitement. She looked up at Mr Kephisto, her eyes shining. "This is exquisite magick."

Mr Kephisto nodded. "Not mine, alas. Well, not all of it. This is Jebediah's work." He pointed at the tree. "What you have here is a rendering from his memory. A physical map of a tree that he considered the most important, not just in Bucklebeare Wood, but in the entire forest that covers that part of Devon and Somerset."

Clarissa drew herself up once more. Something in Mr Kephisto's voice told her this vision was not the end of the magick here. Her stomach fluttered in anticipation and she peered more carefully at the tree.

"Pay attention to the trunk there," Mr Kephisto told them, and Toby scuttled forward to inspect the image closely, hoping to see more squirrels.

Mr Kephisto reached for the vision in front of them. Unlike Clarissa, nothing held his hand back. As Clarissa and Toby watched, he stroked the front of the tree, just once—and gently—from the top where the branches were densest, to the bottom where the roots effervesced above the forest floor.

As his hand swept down the trunk, the bark split apart in six places revealing small holes. Three of the holes—the three at the top—remained dark, like the cavernous eye-holes of ancient skulls, but the other three glowed brightly; red at the bottom, orange above that and yellow above those.

"Is this where the stones belong?" asked Toby, his ears twitching, unsure whether to be anxious or curious.

"I think so." Mr Kephisto nodded sagely.

Clarissa turned about. She'd left the matchbox containing the blue gemstone on the table next to the tea things. Now she picked it up and opened the box again to peer inside. "If this belongs to the tree, who took it away?"

Mr Kephisto shrugged. "I have no idea. When I spoke to Jebediah and drew up the illustration, all of the stones were intact. They are numbered from the bottom. So, the red stone here at the base is The One Stone. The orange stone above it is The Two Stone, and so on."

"Well, that's right!" Clarissa squealed. "When I told Grace Catesby—my old mentor from Ravenswood Hall—about the purple stone, she called it The Six Stone. And she gave me a phone number to call to tell the people on the other end that The Six Stone had been stolen."

"Who did you call?" asked Mr Kephisto.

Clarissa thought back. "It was weird. A really odd conversation. It was a bakery or something. I don't remember."

"Do you still have the number?"

Clarissa widened her eyes. "I'm not sure." She strode towards where her handbag was lying and tipped out the contents on the floor.

Toby rolled his eyes. "We may be some time," he told Mr Kephisto.

Clarissa flipped through the contents of her handbag, before sitting back on her haunches and screwing her nose up. "I can't find it. Perhaps it's at home on my desk. I'll let you know if I come across it. Or I'll get in touch with Catesby and ask her about it."

Mr Kephisto nodded, his face serious. "It is interesting that your mentor knows something about the stones. I'd like to talk to her about that." He pointed at the parchment on the table. "Only Jebediah should have known about this. It was supposed to be a secret."

"I'll pass your information on," Clarissa promised. She made her way back to the tree. It hovered in the air, still growing out of the parchment. It shimmied and sparkled under her renewed inspection.

"What can you tell us about this tree? What are the stones for?"

Mr Kephisto ran his fingers along the writing on the bottom of the parchment. "Jebediah kept it all very close to his chest, and he took the mystery to his grave. He did tell me that as long as the tree was kept secret, nobody would find it and untap its power." Mr Kephisto met Clarissa's eyes. "That was all an incredibly long time ago. So long ago that I'd almost forgotten it myself. Jebediah died assuming that nobody else but me knew about it. Certainly, when I drew the illustration at his behest, all of the stones were in place. They've been removed more recently."

"Somewhere along the line, someone else has found out about it," Toby piped up.

"That much seems obvious," agreed Mr Kephisto. "Grace Catesby and who else, I wonder?"

"Yep." Clarissa's eyes widened. "From what you've said, Jebediah wanted to keep a tight lid on the whereabouts of the tree and the power he thought it yielded, and yet several people have uncovered that secret somehow. We're going to have to assume that Miranda Dervish knows the value of the stones and she's after them too." Clarissa frowned. "That's kind of scary. How has she found out?"

Toby pawed at Clarissa's leg. "And not just

Catesby and The Pointy Woman. Think about it. The stones have been removed from the trunk of the tree. Old Joe had one—"

"And Mrs Crouch had another."

"And they were both hiding them." Toby looked from Clarissa to Mr Kephisto. "So, what did they know about the stones?"

"This raises more questions than answers, certainly." Mr Kephisto stroked his beard. "Because who was it that removed the stones in the first place?"

Clarissa nodded. "And how did they end up in Old Joe's and Mrs Crouch's safekeeping?"

"I hate to mention this, but you're missing something important here," Toby said, and when they both looked at him, he wrinkled his nose in some kind of pseudo-snarl. "We have The Five Stone. The Pointy Woman has The Six Stone..."

Mr Kephisto turned to stare at the tree again. "And three of the stones are still embedded in the trunk."

Clarissa blinked. "So where is The Four Stone?"

Toby growled. "We need to find it before The Pointy Woman does."

Clarissa's stomach sank. "If she doesn't have it already."

CHAPTER TWELVE

"Are you sure you're not breaking the speed limit?" Toby lay on the back seat of Clarissa's car, his paws covering his eyes.

Clarissa glanced in the rear-view mirror. "It's the national speed limit along here, silly." She checked for road signs to make extra sure. She couldn't afford a speeding ticket. The absence of any signs proved her assumption. "Besides. I'm not going *that* fast. I'm doing under fifty."

"It feels like a hundred and fifty," Toby complained, his stomach lurching as she rounded another bend. "I'm sure we're driving on two wheels."

Clarissa snorted, but removed her foot from the accelerator and took her speed down to nearer forty. Toby was right after all. The roads around here were bendy and narrow. It wouldn't pay to career into a tractor when you weren't concentrating. She couldn't imagine her old Nissan would come out of such a meeting too well.

"It's a good job I didn't have any lunch." Toby sat up and gazed out of the window as they sped past hedges and trees. "I'd have lost it by now."

"You had plenty of biscuits," Clarissa pointed out.

"That's all that was on offer. And besides, you had nicer ones. Ones with sugar and cream filling."

"They're very bad for you," Clarissa told him, keeping her face straight. "Too much sugar and you'll end up with diabetes or something equally as horrid."

That didn't sound pleasant to Toby. "Is there sugar in sammiches?"

Clarissa shook her head and rapidly changed through the gears to take a particularly sharp downhill bend. "I expect so. Processed bread. Ham maybe? I don't know really."

Toby gave that some thought. "So sammiches might be a little bit better for you than hooman biscuits?"

Clarissa guffawed. "They might well be."

"That's good to know."

They drove along in companionable silence for a mile or so until Toby couldn't help but mention, "I could really go a sammich right now."

Putting her foot down to build up speed once

more, Clarissa tutted. "I don't have any on me. I didn't know we'd be out this long. I intended to speak to Mr Kephisto, and we'd go home so I could carry on working. But I just thought, while we're out, it might be a good idea to speak to Catesby at our earliest opportunity."

"It's nearly four o'clock," Toby pointed out, nodding at the clock on Clarissa's dashboard. "It's getting late."

"Well, that's the beauty of a boarding school, isn't it? They never close."

"Is it like a kennels then?" Toby shuddered at the thought of the Sun Valley Pet Sanctuary.

Clarissa grunted. "Now that you come to mention it..."

"I'm looking forward to seeing where you grew up."

"And meeting my dear friend Catesby," Clarissa reminded him. "She was a second mother to me, and a good friend when I needed one."

"Will they have sammiches at the school?"

"Catesby might."

Toby settled back in his seat with a satisfied glint in his eye. "Ravenswood must be better than the kennels in that case."

They continued on in silence. Toby, gazing out of a

side window, found that if he simply concentrated on the horizon—as far as he could see it anyway, given they were driving through the woods—his nausea could be held in check. He searched for the horizon among the trees—it didn't move anywhere near as fast as the ground closest to him—and scoured the shadows for deer or squirrels, while allowing his body to relax and move with the vehicle.

In fact, he relaxed so much he almost fell asleep. When Clarissa slowed to take a hard left, the feel of the tyres on the road changed. He sat up straight, eyes wide open, tilting his head this way and that to investigate where they were. Clarissa drove along a rough road, more stone and gravel than tarmac, passing through a huge pair of twisted iron gates. A large building, bigger than anything that Toby had ever seen before, loomed up in front of them.

"Is this a castle?" asked Toby, as Clarissa slotted the car into a parking space.

"No. This is Ravenswood Hall."

Toby ducked his head to stare out of the back window. "Wow-wee! But it looks like a castle."

"It doesn't look like a castle," Clarissa laughed. "It's just an enormous house. Once upon a time it was an Abbey and a Duke lived here. But he came to a sticky end, or so I've been told at any rate. The founder of the school bought it for a pittance. I think she persuaded the Duke's heirs that it was haunted, and to be honest, it probably is." Clarissa pulled on the handbrake and reached for her handbag. "Do you want to stay here or come with me?"

"I want to see inside, of course!" *Sammiches*, he thought to himself.

Clarissa pulled the seat forward and allowed him to jump out, before quickly snapping his lead to his collar.

"I'm not going to run off," he protested.

"This will make sure of that. I can't have you running riot in a school, can I?"

He trotted amiably on the lead beside her as she headed for the main entrance. "It's very quiet, isn't it?" he asked.

"It's the middle of summer, most of the students go home."

Toby looked up at her. "I guess you didn't? When you were here?"

Clarissa pulled a face. "You guess right. I had nowhere to go. Me and a few other students had to stay here all year round. But it was alright." Clarissa sighed. "At least I had Catesby." She smiled down at Toby. "Make sure you behave. But I think she'll love you."

"Of course she'll love me," Toby swaggered along the path beside her. "How could she not?"

He fell silent as they drew closer to the building and the flight of steps that led up to the entrance. The grey stone of the walls and the dozens upon dozens of windows were quite intimidating for a small-ish dog. In spite of his confident appearance, Toby was a little worried about what Catesby would think of him. Given how much the housemistress had meant to Clarissa, he felt it was important to make a good impression.

They climbed the steps and Clarissa pushed the door open, leading him through into the grand entrance and a large foyer at the foot of the impressive curving staircase. Toby paused, his head swivelling, staring open-mouthed at the grandeur on view; the marble of the staircase, the tiling on the floor, the huge gilt-framed portraits hanging on the walls.

To the left was a small wooden bench. He recalled how Clarissa, on the day they'd first met, had related to him, that as an eight-year-old, she had waited on such a bench on the night her 'Auntie' Miranda had come to collect her from her cold and empty house when her parents had failed to come home.

Clarissa gave the bench a hard stare for a long

moment, before squaring her shoulders and lifting her chin.

"This way," she told him, and he skipped alongside her as she headed for a door in the corner.

This door opened into a small hallway with a number of additional doors off it. The one closest to them stood ajar.

"Hello? Catesby?" Clarissa stepped inside and pulled up short. "Oh."

The room, obviously Catesby's study at some stage, had been cleared. The large battered desk took centre stage on the wooden floor, while a pair of tattered armchairs, the upholstery badly stained on the armrests, had been pushed in front of the window. There were dozens of bookshelves but they were all empty. Rectangular marks on the walls clearly demonstrated where posters and framed photos and paintings had once hung, and an ancient filing cabinet stood idly in the corner, one of its drawers, now empty, gaped open.

But of Catesby there was no sign.

Clarissa took a few steps towards the empty desk. She'd never known the cramped and cluttered study tidy, let alone empty. "What on earth—"

"May I be of assistance?"

A deep voice from the hallway startled them both. They swivelled to face the newcomer at the same time.

A tall, thin woman with long black hair and brilliant blue eyes regarded them suspiciously. Clarissa had never seen her before.

"I was looking for Catesby," Clarissa gestured around the empty office.

The woman smiled, but without warmth. Her pupils were black chips of granite in an icy sea of blue. "And who might you be?"

Clarissa stepped forward and offered a hand. "I'm Clarissa Page. I studied here. Catesby—that is Miss Catesby—was my housemistress."

The woman regarded Clarissa's hand with unconcealed contempt and made no move to shake it.

"I popped by to say hello," Clarissa said, her voice beginning to falter in the face of the other woman's continued disinterest.

"Miss Catesby has gone on sabbatical," the other woman told Clarissa, looking down and curling her lip as Toby pulled towards her to sniff around her feet.

"She has?" Clarissa frowned and pulled Toby away. "Only, I saw her just a few weeks ago and she didn't say anything about going away."

"It was a recent decision. The opportunity arose and she jumped at the chance." The woman's eyes bore holes into Clarissa's skull. "We encourage that sort of thing at Ravenswood, as you know."

Clarissa nodded slowly, uncertain of the veracity of such a sweeping statement. "I'm sorry, I don't believe we've met?" she said.

"Dr Ermintrude Chevalier," the woman replied, attempting another smile but only succeeding in sneering this time. "I've been installed as housemistress in Miss Catesby's absence."

"I see." Clarissa couldn't prevent the note of despondency from entering her voice. Toby had wandered back in the woman's direction, his nose busy around her feet.

Dr Chevalier stepped away from him, and Clarissa pulled him back towards her once more. "Temporarily, of course." Dr Chevalier's eyes swept around the empty office. "I'll be moving my things in here shortly. Is there anything I can help you with?"

Clarissa started. *Goodness, no.* "I erm—no, it's fine. I just—" she indicated Toby, "—we just wanted to say hi. I was passing." She nodded vigorously as though that made the lie more believable. "Is there a forwarding address? Could I perhaps get in touch with Catesby some other way?"

Dr Chevalier shook her head. "Unfortunately not.

She's on a private retreat. Not reachable for several months."

"Several months?" Clarissa couldn't believe what she was hearing. This was a disaster.

"I'm afraid so." Dr Chevalier stood back to allow Clarissa to step through on her way out to the main lobby. "I'm sorry I can't be of any further assistance to you, but now I'm afraid I have to get on."

"Of course." Clarissa led Toby out, preceding the woman into the grand entrance. "I'm sorry to have disturbed you."

"Oh, don't worry about it." And now there appeared to be a little warmth in her tone. "Past students are always welcome at Ravenswood, as you know."

"Thank you," Clarissa nodded, and made her way to the entrance.

Dr Chevalier's voice followed her. "But perhaps next time, leave the dog in the car?"

"The absolute cheek of it." Toby's indignance rankled with Clarissa, who was feeling a tad bad-tempered herself.

"You know what would be nice?" she asked, snapping her seatbelt into place. "Is if you'd consider for a moment someone else other than yourself."

Toby pouted. "I only meant—"

Clarissa glowered at him and he clamped his mouth shut, hurriedly lying down on the back seat. He decided not to mention to Clarissa that she hadn't attached his harness to his dog seatbelt in case she gave him another ear-bashing, and just gave her a little wary side-eye instead.

She started the engine and reversed out of her space harder than was necessary. The beat-up old Nissan's wheels scattered stone chips into the ornamental borders that surrounded the car park as Clarissa slammed into second and wound the old car up. But she could only drive like that for a moment. The road was too pot-holed to withstand any kind of speed without damaging the chassis or the wheel rims.

She drove more slowly through the iron gates and onto the main approach to Ravenswood. Occasionally she glanced in the rear-view mirror, her forehead creased, but she never met Toby's eye. He figured she was watching her old school fade into the distance.

Once they were out of view of the school, Clarissa pulled into a make-shift layby, not much more than an inlet that allowed two vehicles to pass safely on the narrow road.

She yanked on the handbrake and left the engine idling, slumped over the steering wheel, hiding her face.

"Are you alright?" Toby asked, peering round her seat, and reaching out a paw to touch her tentatively on the arm.

He heard her take a deep breath in response, and clearing her throat she sat up, blinking at him.

"I'm fine. Sorry. What an awful woman, eh? I shouldn't have taken it out on you."

He nudged her bare arm with his cold wet nose. "That's alright. I probably deserved it."

"Oh, you did." Clarissa laughed and reached for her handbag to extract her phone and a bag of treats. She offered him a snack and he took it gratefully. It must have been absolutely *years* since he'd last eaten.

"I'm worried about Catesby," she said, and began to thumb through the contacts list on her phone. "If she'd been intending to take a sabbatical anywhere then I'm sure she would have mentioned that to me the last time I saw her."

"Dr Chevalier said it was a sudden decision," Toby ventured, but he hadn't liked the woman so it wouldn't surprise him if she'd been telling porky-pies.

"Dr Chevalier said two things. A sabbatical *and* a retreat. And while I'm sure that neither of these is inconsistent with the other, it didn't ring true to me." Clarissa located Catesby's number on her phone. "I'm absolutely certain that had she been intending to go on a retreat and didn't want to be bothered by the outside world, she would have informed everyone that's what she was doing so that we wouldn't need to worry." Clarissa jabbed at the screen. "What she wouldn't have done, is simply disappeared."

Clarissa held the phone to her ear and waited. Toby could hear a faint ringing tone that went on and on for an eternity. Eventually Clarissa gave up listening and thumbed the screen.

Sighing in exasperation, she turned in her seat and regarded Toby. "That's a rotten coincidence, all things considered, don't you think?"

"I do," he said. "And you know what else is a coincidence?"

"Go on..."

"Dr Chevalier's feet smelled like The Pointy Woman's feet. Musty oldness. Like cellars."

Clarissa grimaced. "Of dark fusty places that don't see the light of day?" she asked, remembering how he'd described Miranda Dervish.

"Yes. Of something not nice. Old books. But not like Mr Kephisto's bookshop." He warmed to his theme, "because that smells like joy and knowledge and escape and happy places." Clarissa's brow furrowed, not understanding how escape or a happy place could have a fragrance attached to it. Toby continued, undaunted by Clarissa's expression. "The Pointy Woman smells of despair and gloom and husky ancientness."

"And Dr Chevalier had the same scent?"

"Exactly the same."

"Hmm." Clarissa turned forwards, staring absently out of the window and tapping her fingers on the steering wheel.

Toby stood on the back seat waiting for her to say something profound, but when she didn't, he nudged her with his cold nose. She jumped a little and came back to the present.

"Are you thinking about sammiches?"

Clarissa rolled her eyes. Toby had a one-track mind. "No. I'm not thinking about my stomach at all. I take it you are."

"I am now." Toby caught her eye in the rear-view mirror. "Maybe we'll think better on a full tummy."

Clarissa, who had eaten far too many biscuits at Mr Kephisto's bookshop, wasn't entirely sure she'd ever be hungry again. She slipped the car into first gear and released the handbrake. They rolled slowly forward, navigating the potholes in the road.

"You know, we're not far from The Blackdown Hills here. If we follow this road out and cross over the motorway, we should find the road into the forest on the other side.

Toby gazed out of the side window. All he could see were trees. The faster they went, the more of a blur they became. It made his head spin. "I thought this was a forest?"

"It is a forest, but it's a different forest." Clarissa put her foot down again as they hit a better piece of road.

"So many forests. So many trees."

Clarissa glanced back at him. "What do you reckon? Can you hold out for dinner for a while longer?"

"While we investigate the other forest that's like this forest but is a different forest, you mean?"

Clarissa snickered and shook her head. "You can be such a sarcastic little so-and-so at times," she smiled. "Yes. That's what I mean."

Toby wagged his tail with enthusiasm. "I'm always up for a walk and a bit of an explore, you know me."

CHAPTER THIRTEEN

"I'm really not sure this was such a good idea." Clarissa had stopped the car and had her iPad out to try and search for an online map that would show them where they were. She poked the screen in exasperation. "Why can't I get a signal?" she groaned. "And where are all the bloomin' road signs?"

Toby's head revolved on his shoulders as he glanced through all the windows. They'd been driving for what felt like hours, although Clarissa reckoned it had been forty minutes. Exploring the forest on foot was one thing; driving through it in a car was something else entirely.

Boring.

All those delicious smells going begging, all those squirrels he could be chasing, all the leaves he could be kicking up.

The problem appeared to be, not to put too fine a

point on it, that Clarissa had managed to get them lost. All the roads here looked the same. Every now and then they would come across a crossroads and would slow down to navigate it. Clarissa would search for a sign to tell her what her options were, and invariably there wasn't one.

"You know what? I saw a programme on the television once that said that during the Second World War, the government saw fit to remove all the road signs in rural areas, and that way if the enemy made it ashore, they would get lost."

"Really?" Toby asked, quite astounded at the notion. Humans were handicapped by their lack of orienteering skills, in his opinion. He had no need to rely on sight because his ears and his nose were far superior.

Although of late, his eyesight had definitely been sharpening. He leaned forward and snuck a peep at Clarissa's tablet. A small wheel in the corner spun and spun, but nothing else seemed to be happening.

"Oooh! I almost had a signal there!" Clarissa waited a moment, staring at the screen hopefully. Eventually, she chucked the device on to the passenger seat. "I give up. Rotten thing. We might as well head home. It's nearly dinnertime anyway."

Dinner sounded good to Toby. "If you don't know

where we are, how will we get home?"

Clarissa ducked her head and squinted in the direction of the sun. "There," she pointed. "Do you see? If we head in the direction the sun is setting, we'll be going west. We just need to hang a left at some stage and that should take us home, or near enough." Clarissa chewed her lip. "Well, eventually, anyway."

She started the engine once more. "I'm sure that if we can reach a main road, or what passes for a main road in this part of the sticks, then we'll find a road sign somewhere."

"You hope." Toby stared into the trees on his left-hand side. A sizeable common grey squirrel stood on the path, looking his way. It needed chasing. "Maybe all of civilisation has disappeared. Maybe we're destined to drive round and round The Forest of Doom forever."

"We can't do that, fortunately, because I don't have enough petrol."

"It'll just be me, you and that squizzel over there." Toby blithely ignored her rational appraisal of the situation, and observed the squirrel as it stood tall on its back legs and lifted a paw.

Was it beckoning to him?

Clarissa stretched her neck. "Squirrel. Right. Ready?"

Toby, still looking through the window, watched as the butch squirrel beckoned him, using its whole arm. It scampered back a few paces, and made exactly the same movement again.

*It **is** beckoning to me,* Toby decided.

"Erm, Clarissa?" Toby nudged the back of her seat. "We need to get out of the car."

Clarissa turned her head and sighed in exasperation. "Can't you wait? I'm sure we'll be home soon."

Toby watched as the squirrel retreated another few metres before turning back to stare at him, its black eyes shining bright. It lifted its furry arm and beckoned once more.

Further along the path he spotted another pair of squirrels darting out of the undergrowth. They too sat back on their haunches and looked his way.

Three squirrels watching him. That seemed unusual.

"No," he repeated with fresh determination. "We *really* need to get out."

Clarissa spotted the squirrels as soon as she stepped out of the car. She reached inside to clip Toby's lead to his collar.

He moaned, "I don't need to be on a lead."

"What's this about?" she demanded. "I'm not letting you run free so you can spend the rest of the evening chasing squirrels. We've more important matters to attend to."

"Trust me," he told her as he jumped out of the back. "I think we may be addressing them right now." He glanced along the path. The squirrels had all remained in place. They squatted on the earth watching him.

Waiting for him to make a move?

Or follow them?

"What do you mean?" Clarissa locked the car and wrapped one end of the lead around her hand. Toby had already started to pull. "Hold your horses!"

Toby ignored her instruction and dragged her forwards. To any casual observer it would have looked as though he was straining to get at the squirrels.

"Toby!" Clarissa complained.

He planted himself solidly on the path and gazed up at her beseechingly. "Please let me off, I need to talk to the squizzels."

"Squirrels," Clarissa corrected him. "Is 'talk' just a euphemism for chase and kill? That's what I'm wondering."

"Not at all. You have my word." He made his best

puppy dog eyes at her and finally she relented, bending down to set him free.

Instantly, he took to his heels and trotted towards the squirrels. "Toby!" Clarissa bellowed after him, but she needn't have worried. The two squirrels at the rear regarded the dog warily, but the one nearest to him merely stood its ground, his or her demeanour remaining perfectly calm.

He pulled up in front of the first squirrel. "Well met," he said, remembering Mad Mabel's greeting to him.

"Indeed." The squirrel, his voice a little high and squeaky, scrutinised the dog with its bright button eyes. "Or at least we hope so." He tipped his head back as Clarissa caught up with Toby, and gave her a similar once over. "Are we all here now?"

"It's just me and Clarissa," Toby confirmed.

The squirrel nodded once and spun around. His tail flicked back at them and he began to scamper along the path. The other squirrels remained where they were until they had passed, then fell in behind them. While Toby simply gambolled along, easily keeping up with them, Clarissa had to break into a run.

"What's going on?" Clarissa called. "Are you talking to the squirrels?"

Toby paused long enough so that they could run

together. "I am, as it happens. I saw the big one from the car window. He looked as though he was calling to us."

Clarissa, breathing hard as she pounded along the rough path, could hardly believe her ears. "Toby. Have you ever spoken to any other wild animals before?"

"I don't believe so. Just cats and dogs. Never a squizzel."

"Do you not find it odd that they've suddenly started communicating with you?" Clarissa panted.

"Not at all. Maybe they just never had anything to say to me before."

Although reasonably fit, Clarissa struggled to keep up the pace. Eventually, after a few minutes of flat-out running, she slowed to a grinding halt and doubled over, her hands on her knees, fighting to get her breath.

Toby waited alongside her, exchanging glances with the squirrels further along the path, who had also pulled up. When she could walk and speak again, Clarissa straightened and clutched her side. "I've got a stitch," she lamented.

Toby had needed stitches once. He'd cut himself on a glass bottle in the park and the vet had stitched the gash in his leg. The stitches had hurt more than the injury itself. But Clarissa didn't appear to be bleeding.

Humans were odd things. Perhaps she was bleeding internally.

"Oh dear," Toby said. "Hopefully we're not far away from where we need to be. Perhaps the squizzels have a doctor."

Clarissa raised her eyebrows. It was easy to forget at times that Toby's world view—as a canine—differed to hers. Did he really imagine that squirrels possessed a medical system? The Squirrel Health Service?

She snorted and waved him on, jogging slowly after the animals as they led her deeper and deeper into the forest. Every now and then they would stop, politely allowing her to rest. The squirrels spoke among themselves and Toby would circle Clarissa, waiting for her to recover.

Then on they would go again.

They must have been running, jogging and walking for forty minutes when finally, the squirrels led Clarissa and Toby into a clearing. Several large trees had been felled here at some time in the past, and the stumps made for perfect seating. Clarissa collapsed onto one and mopped her brow. Fortunately, the sun had started to drop towards the horizon and the air was cooling rapidly. Twilight wouldn't be long.

Clarissa gathered her strength and her thoughts. The squirrels had disappeared. Had she and Toby really followed these woodland creatures into the centre of a forest she didn't know at all? And at this time of day?

What had she been thinking?

Toby, panting a little—perhaps more to show sympathy with her condition than his own tiredness—collapsed alongside her. "This is exciting, isn't it?"

"What are we doing here, Toby? Where have your friends gone?" Clarissa asked.

Something hit the ground near her foot with a soft plunking sound, alarming her. She brushed at her hair in case spiders—or worse—were tumbling out of the branches above her head, but remained sitting on her stump. She scoured the forest floor around her feet for the offending article, while Toby sniffed helpfully around too.

A sudden rustling from above had her on her feet quickly enough. She started in surprise. A long row of squirrels were perching on a branch above her head.

Clarissa opened her mouth to speak and closed it again. She had never seen so many squirrels in one place before. There must have been twenty or so on that one branch, and when she widened her line of vision, she spotted dozens and dozens of others, also lined up on the branches above, all of them peering down on her and Toby.

"Clarissa," Toby broke into her thoughts.

"Have you seen these guys?" Clarissa whispered. She lifted a tremulous finger and pointed at the branch nearest her. The squirrels twitched, fighting to inhabit their personal squirrel space or at least keep their balance, and squeaked to each other. Given how animated they were, gesturing her way and chirruping, she wondered if they were discussing her.

"Clarissa?" Toby tried again.

She spun around. Toby stood alongside another tree stump. The squirrels they had followed through the forest had returned—although to be fair, Clarissa wasn't sure she could tell them apart—and climbed on top of this one to use it as a stage. The three young squirrels flanked an older friend, with mottled, moth-eaten fur and a less bushy tail than the others. His or her eyes were dim, as though failing, but it still regarded Clarissa with a keen intelligence.

"The squizzels would like to talk to you, but they appreciate you don't have the capacity to understand them," Toby said.

Clarissa raised her eyebrows, unsure how to respond.

One of the younger squirrels squeaked. Toby heard him out, nodded, and turned back to Clarissa. "They want you to know that they don't blame you for your lack of ability." Toby made a gruff-sounding barking noise, that might have been amusement. "I've explained that I'm happy to translate."

"I see." Clarissa decided she might as well go with it. What choice did she have? The whole situation seemed oddly surreal to her. Ten years at Ravenswood had not prepared her for talking squirrels, that much was certain. "Alright."

The older squirrel moved to the edge of its tree stump. It cocked its head in Toby's direction to check the dog was paying attention, before pivoting to stare directly at Clarissa. It raised its cute little fists and began to communicate in a series of complicated but melodic squeaks and chirps, barks and purrs.

Clarissa listened entranced, and almost fooled herself into believing she could understand what the old squirrel was saying. Toby kept up a steady stream of dialogue as he translated.

"This squizzel is known as..." Toby checked with the squirrel, "Grappletwigs. She is the First Lady of the Blackdown Hills Squizzel Community. These are her sons, Nibbles—" Toby indicated the butch squirrel who had first caught his attention, "Fidgetchin and Bundlecote. They're twins apparently. She is pleased to make your acquaintance and hopes you will enjoy your time here with the Blackdown Hills Squizzels."

Toby listened carefully and started again. "Lady Grappletwigs tells me that it is unusual for squizzels to seek out the company of hoomans and dogs." He shot the elderly squirrel a look. "I can't think why—"

Grappletwigs swatted at the dog with a balled-up squirrel fist, and squeaked at him some more.

"Okay, okay. Hmpf." Toby huffed. "Apparently canines are the bane of any squizzel's life. I've been told I'm not to chase any of them ever again."

"In no uncertain terms, by the sound of it," Clarissa smirked.

Toby nodded. "You're not kidding. The wrath of Squizzelkind will be upon me."

Jovial chittering from the branches above Clarissa's head reminded her of the sheer force of numbers gathered about the clearing. Clearly they found Grappletwigs' handling of Toby hilarious.

Toby continued, "But in all seriousness, Grappletwigs says she has led you here today for a particular reason. She received a communication from old ones." Toby looked puzzled. "Which old ones?" he asked Grappletwigs.

She twittered at him. "From *The* Old Ones," Toby corrected himself. "The ones that came before. The ones who have passed."

Clarissa drew in a sharp breath. "*The* Old Ones?" She clamped her fingers in front of her mouth.

She'd been so blasé. How could she have made light of what was happening here?

With that one phrase, her view of this forest altered dramatically. She peered around at the twisted trunks of trees and the weighted canopy above her head. She paid proper attention to the moss on rocks that had littered this place since time immemorial, she took in the lichen that wrapped itself around fallen trees—those warriors of the forest—like nurturing shrouds. She recognised this was not simply a parcel of land populated by trees and comedy squirrels, but actually the heart of an ancient site of great importance.

She stood in the place that Jebediah Hornbrook had once cultivated and nurtured.

The realisation punched her in the gut. She lurched forwards and dropped to her knees in front of Grappletwigs. The Old Ones were sending Clarissa a message. It behoved her to listen.

"Tell me," she said.

Grappletwigs regarded Clarissa with sombre eyes.

"Now you know," she said, Toby translating.

Clarissa pressed her lips together in a solemn line. "I do," she agreed. "It is an honour to be summoned here."

"Perhaps the honour is ours. Perhaps it is not. Either way, it was not my decision to bring you here." Grappletwigs twitched her threadbare tail. "The Old Ones will it, and their will must, therefore, be done."

Clarissa glanced around the clearing, looking more carefully at the fallen trees around her. Her heart beat a little faster. "Jebediah Hornbrook's tree?" she asked. Could it have been felled?

"Is a little further into the forest. I will take you there when night falls. It has long been enchanted. Before his death, Jebediah Hornbrook made sure that it could never be found. It can only be seen under the rays of a full moon. And even then, the seeker must be accompanied by one of Jebediah's chosen few."

Clarissa breathed a little more easily. Tonight, the moon was full. "I see."

Grappletwigs chirruped in annoyance. "You see nothing. That's the problem with you humans. You imagine you have all the answers."

Clarissa ducked her head. "I apologise. I didn't mean—"

"If it were left to me, I'd ensure nobody visited the

site, but the damage has been done."

Panic began to pluck at Clarissa's intestines once more. "Damage? What's happened?"

"One of Jebediah's chosen few betrayed us all."

"How? What happened?"

Grappletwigs narrowed her eyes at all the squirrels sitting on branches in the trees around them. She shook her head. "I cannot talk freely." She indicated Clarissa's tree stump. "Rest now. Nibbles will show you a spring where you can quench your thirst. I will return at moonrise. We will venture to the site together."

Clarissa endured a nervous wait.

The shadows grew longer and longer until the light failed altogether. She sat on her tree stump, Toby snoozing at her feet. She envied his ability to do this. How easy for him to simply switch off. For her part, she started at every noise, every branch cracking, every shuffle of leaves in the distance.

As night fell, the look and sound and feel of the forest around them changed. The twittering of bird song at dusk, so jubilant and melancholy, faded to silence. Where there had been a distinct lack of breeze before, now it built up, and the leaves in the canopy above their heads began to whisper and dance.

Clarissa considered giving up. "How much longer?" she asked aloud.

Toby stirred. "Patience," he said. "Grappletwigs will return. She promised."

And, a little later, return she did, with only Nibbles for company.

Clarissa jumped to her feet as Grappletwigs hopped into the clearing. The moon shone large and round, clearly visible through the higher branches of the trees.

"I have banished the rest of my scurry for the time being, and the word is out. Walk with me."

In spite of her age, Grappletwigs made good time and Clarissa had to walk quickly to remain by her side. Toby followed behind them, and Nibbles brought up the rear.

Clarissa had imagined that they would locate some mysterious hidden path, but they continued to follow a track that had probably been lain down many centuries previously. There was nothing obviously mystical or magickal about it, no fairy lights hanging from the trees, no other indication of anything special.

Except with every step Clarissa took, with every breath in, she became increasingly lightheaded. It wasn't a lack of oxygen, more that the air available to breathe became ever purer. In no time at all Grappletwigs had led them into another clearing, this one smaller than the last, the surroundings devoid of all forest detritus. No fallen trees, no stumps, no large branches or brambles or rocks cluttering up the place. Just a smallish circle, so clean that it might even have been swept clear of leaves and chestnut casings.

Clarissa turned slowly around. She should have been disappointed. She'd expected to see Jebediah's tree, and having seen Mr Kephisto's drawings she would probably have recognised it anywhere, but quite obviously it wasn't here.

And yet, all was not lost.

She could feel the presence of something mighty and wonderful, and Toby's reaction told her he could sense it too. His head rotated, his ears pricked, his eyes burned into the centre of the clearing.

"Do you have to call it?" Clarissa asked Grappletwigs.

Grappletwigs lifted her arms. "It is ever present. But only those who are blessed with the sight can see it."

"I would like to see it," Clarissa said.

"And you shall." Grappletwigs gestured at Toby as he translated her words to Clarissa. "You both shall.

But know this, from hereon in you are honour-bound to protect the location of Jebediah's Beech Tree and all knowledge relating to its existence. You must swear this on your lives."

"I do swear," Clarissa said, touching her heart.

"And I," Toby added, his tail drooping at a solemn angle.

"Very well." Grappletwigs nodded at Nibbles and he scurried up the nearest tree, as nimble as the wind. He disappeared for a moment. In lightning fast time he reappeared and bounced to the ground once more, clutching what looked to be a beech nut between his front paws. He handed it over to his mother, bowed respectfully and scampered away, through the trees and out of sight.

Clarissa, Toby and Grappletwigs were alone.

"Stand back," the elderly squirrel ordered, and Toby and Clarissa retreated to the shelter of the nearest tree.

"*Kommana sureeta chirrah levitato medaleo. Burnificia garganta!*" Grappletwigs shouted, and threw the beech nut into the centre of the clearing. It exploded like a firework. A burst of gold glitter shot violently into the air, reaching ten or twelve feet above Clarissa's head. She ducked and winced, looking up at the sparks, expecting them to rain down on her.

But they continued only to rise.

The cloud of sparks at the top of the rising column began to spread out, taking the shape of a tall beech tree with a full skeleton of branches and a wild mop of leaves. Clarissa and Toby tilted their heads back to watch it grow and grow, and then grow some more.

"Wow!" Toby gasped. Here was a magick the like of which he'd never seen before. He gazed up at the tree with wide shining eyes.

"Wow indeed," Clarissa whispered, equally as entranced by the powerful energy that rippled in the air around them, and by the sheer scale of the tree. This beech tree appeared to be the spitting image of the one in Mr Kephisto's drawing and, semi-transparent, it shimmered with light.

Grappletwigs hopped towards it and lay her hands on the bark, then twisted her head and lay an ear against the trunk, as though listening for a heartbeat. After a moment she sighed with satisfaction and pulled away.

"It is still strong. It draws on the blood of the earth and nourishes the atmosphere. It lives."

Clarissa stepped towards the tree, faltering, unsure whether she should approach. Grappletwigs beckoned her closer. Toby joined her as Clarissa crouched next to the squirrel and lay her hand on the trunk. The tree seemed to melt beneath her touch. Her hand grew warm, tingling with pins and needles, but not painfully.

"Stroke the trunk," Grappletwigs ordered, and Clarissa, remembering Mr Kephisto doing the very same thing, stood. She stretched on tiptoes, reaching as high as she was able, before running her hand lightly down the trunk, feeling the lumps and bumps of the bark and moss beneath her palm, all the way to the ground.

Just as she'd witnessed in Mr Kephisto's study, the trunk rippled like water and split gently apart, revealing small holes in six places. And just as she'd seen before, three of the holes—the three at the top—remained dark, like cavernous eye holes. The other three winked open, light spilling around the clearing and illuminating the surroundings in glorious technicolour. A red flame-shaped stone at the bottom, an orange sun in the middle, and a yellow half-moon shaped stone above those.

Clarissa cupped her hand around the nearest eye. Red light bled through her fingers. "What is the meaning of this tree?" she asked Grappletwigs.

"It is a source of great natural magick. By itself, it is the heart of the forest. A giver of life and hope, of love and truth. But only when it is shared by all and with all. Only when it is shared with each and every living creature within a thousand miles or more."

Clarissa reached out to the nearest empty hole. The one where The Four Stone should be. "So if nobody knows about it, all is well?" she asked.

"Correct," said the squirrel, her dull eyes following Clarissa's hand as it caressed the hole.

Something in the squirrel's tone caused Clarissa's heart to beat a little faster. "And if it isn't shared equally?" Clarissa asked.

"The problem with Jebediah's Beech Tree is that once it has been discovered, as with all things, its power can be harvested. Someone can claim ownership."

"Completely erroneously." Clarissa's breath seemed to stick in her throat.

"Exactly." Grappletwigs nodded, a slow, despairing movement. "With all the stones intact, this tree has a power beyond measure, and woe betide us if someone harnesses it to use for ill."

"Because?"

"They will have access to magickal powers far greater than any the world has historically ever known."

"But didn't you already say that one of Jebediah Hornbrook's chosen ones betrayed the location of the tree?" Clarissa sucked in a breath, dreading Grappletwigs' response. "Someone does know about it. We'd already worked that out."

"Someone did betray us, and yes, a few more people now know about the tree." Grappletwigs face wore a mask of grief. "The one who betrayed us gave his knowledge away under duress admittedly, but it was an unforgivable betrayal nonetheless."

"Has someone accessed the tree?" Toby asked, his ears flat against his head, his eyes wide. "Was it The Pointy Woman?"

Clarissa's mind raced. "No," she shook her head, frowning at Grappletwigs. "She couldn't have come here and taken the stones, because she's been looking for them."

The old squirrel wrinkled her nose. "You are bright, my young witch friend."

Clarissa warmed to her idea. "The stones were removed from the tree to protect them?"

"Indeed. Many years ago. And three of them have been returned," the squirrel confirmed.

"But in order to harness the full power of the tree, all the stones have to be in place?" Clarissa guessed.

"That's right," Grappletwigs nodded.

Toby finally understood. "So, The Pointy Woman knows about the tree and she's trying to collect the rest of the stones so she can be the one who harnesses the power."

"Yes." Clarissa frowned. "She's already a third of the way there. She has The Six Stone."

Toby nudged her. "But we have The Five Stone."

"It's in a matchbox in my bag!" Clarissa gasped in horror. "I left it in the car."

Grappletwigs squeaked her laughter, a high-pitched squealy squirrelly giggle. "Don't worry," she said, "I have sentinels watching your vehicle. It is well protected."

"I could get the stone and return it to you," Clarissa offered.

"No need. We set the stones free on purpose. They should only be returned when the time is right."

Toby wagged his tail in excitement. "Are you setting a trap? If you have all the remaining stones together, you can do that. She will come here, The Pointy Woman. She will want to add her stone to the others. When she does that, we can catch her."

Grappletwigs held her paws out to the dog. Toby stepped closer so that she could rest her squirrel hands on his muzzle. "You are a wise hound. This is our exact intention. It is why we have called upon you and your human."

Clarissa cocked her head as Toby translated for

her. "What do you need us to do?" she asked.

"We want you to locate The Four Stone before the Dervish woman does. When you have that one, come back to us."

Clarissa blanched. "That's a big ask. I'm not sure where to start looking."

"I understand." Grappletwigs smiled, oddly unphased by this. "But The Old Ones have assured us that you and Toby will find a way. We trust you to do so."

Clarissa raised her eyes to the skies in wonder. "Why us? Why do you—and they—think we can do this?

"You were chosen because of your grandfather."

"Old Joe?" asked Toby.

"Many years ago, The Old Ones let him into the secret of Jebediah's Beech Tree."

Clarissa frowned, thinking of all the paperwork she'd searched through after Old Joe's death. There had been no mention of any of the stones, or Jebediah Hornbrook or a Magickal Beech Tree. "Why did they want to do that?"

Grappletwig's tail twitched. "After the betrayal of the tree's location, we needed to take urgent steps. Your grandfather was let in on the secret because it was him we entrusted to remove the stones."

CHAPTER FOURTEEN

The following afternoon, Clarissa sat alongside Mr Kephisto in the hospital waiting room. They put their heads together and spoke in hushed voices. Clarissa had filled him in on Grace Catesby's mysterious disappearance from Ravenswood Hall, and her encounter with the squirrels. She'd then asked him for assistance in locating the final stone.

"I'll do what I can, but to be honest, I had no idea the stones were missing. When I spoke to Jebediah, the stones were all intact."

Clarissa regarded the old wizard thoughtfully. She pondered again on how long ago he had spoken to Jebediah. She had a sneaking suspicion it had to have been a very, very long time ago. How that could be possible, she didn't have the faintest notion.

"This is a most intriguing mystery," Mr Kephisto

continued, his voice ringing with excitement rather than unease.

Clarissa blew her cheeks out. "Albeit a deadly one. My grandfather is dead and poor Mrs Crouch still hasn't woken up from her coma."

Mr Kephisto's eyes sparkled. "That's why we're here, my dear."

"In his last letter to me, my grandfather spoke of me being on a journey. He said something like, each of us has a path to follow, and although he could no longer protect me, he knew I could succeed. But he also said the journey would be daunting." Clarissa pulled a wry face. "Well, it certainly has been so far."

"You have to locate the final stone before Miranda Dervish. Let's hope she has no idea you're looking for it too."

That thought hadn't occurred to Clarissa. She glanced around the waiting room uneasily. They were on the Intensive Care floor, and fortunately there were only four other people sharing the room. A middle-aged couple, strain on their tired faces, and a pale-looking woman and her teenage son. He pored over his mobile phone and ignored everyone else. The pale woman flicked idly through a magazine. The other couple clasped hands and whispered to each other, showing no interest in Clarissa and Mr Kephisto.

"I have absolutely no idea where to start," Clarissa sighed. "I'll look back through my grandfather's paperwork and utilise Toby to search the house top to bottom to see if I can find it, but my instinct says it's a long shot."

Mr Kephisto nodded. "And I'll run a search of my archives and cross-reference anything I have regarding The Blackdown Hills, Jebediah Hornbrook and Joseph Silverwind, and we'll see where that gets us."

"Every piece of information, no matter how small, will help us." Clarissa stared at the closed door, willing a doctor or a nurse to come through and give them some news. She'd rung Mr Kephisto first thing this morning and he'd asked her to meet at the hospital for two.

That had meant leaving Toby by himself—and she imagined that, by now, he would be levitating pencils and dog treats or trying to chat to squirrels in the back garden—and driving into the city, not knowing what to expect.

"One important thing to remember," Mr Kephisto was saying, "is that Mrs Crouch had one of the stones."

Clarissa nodded without any enthusiasm. Mrs Crouch couldn't communicate with them. "If there had been another stone in her house, I'm fairly certain

Toby would have found it. His abilities are increasing at a rather alarming rate."

"I'm not disagreeing," Mr Kephisto said, "but you're missing the point. If Joseph gave Mrs Crouch a stone, there's a strong chance he placed the missing stone with somebody else he trusted. We just have to work out who that person might have been."

"Huh," Clarissa huffed. Why hadn't she thought of that? "That makes a lot of sense. I'll look into it and try and work out who his friends were."

The door opened and a nurse in dark blue scrubs poked her head around. "Mr Crouch?" she asked.

Mr Kephisto jumped to his feet. "Yes. That's me."

"Mrs Crouch's brother-in-law?"

"That's right. I'm her only remaining relative. This is my granddaughter."

Clarissa frowned in surprise. He'd *lied* to the nurses at the reception desk about who he was?

"Would you like to come this way, please?" They followed her out into the corridor. The name on her badge said Theresa. "I'm so pleased that Mrs Crouch can finally have some visitors. It's been an awfully lonely time for her. I do so hate it when we can't locate close family," she said.

"Has there been any change?" asked Clarissa, crossing her fingers.

Theresa shook her head. "Sadly not. All we can do is wait."

She led them into a small side room. Mrs Crouch lay on the only bed, small and pale and still, beneath a blanket. Several machines beeped quietly to themselves, monitoring her vitals. The blind had been pulled down over the window to block out the bright sunshine.

The nurse leaned over to check on Mrs Crouch before straightening up and smiling at Mr Kephisto. "I'll leave you to it."

"Thank you." Mr Kephisto dropped his head as though in prayer and Theresa took her leave. When the wizard was certain they were alone, he lifted his chin. "Lock the door," he told Clarissa.

Clarissa raised her eyebrows. There had to be a wide variety of reasons for why locking the door might not be a good idea, but she did it anyway.

Mr Kephisto walked swiftly around to the other side of Mrs Crouch's bed and lifted one of her hands. Clarissa assumed he had to be taking her pulse, but the way he held her hand, rubbing the palm with his thumb, seemed a slightly unorthodox way of measuring someone's vital signs. He turned Mrs Crouch's arm over and scanned her skin closely from her fingertips to the crease in the elbow. Then he flipped her hand over again and studied the back.

His breath caught. "There." He pointed at the faintest green traces deeply embedded in the thumbnail. "Do you see?"

Clarissa carefully took Mrs Crouch's hand from him and scrutinised where he'd indicated. "I see it. It isn't paint or something like that? Dye maybe?"

"Look more closely and you'll see the colour is actually in the nail itself." Clarissa nodded her assent. "Check the other hand."

She did so and found more traces there. "And on the index finger, here. What is it?"

"Evidence of a toxic enchantment. A physical curse."

"Really?" Clarissa rubbed a hand against her chest. "That does not sound good."

"If it was Miranda, she probably intended to kill. Luckily for us, for some reason she couldn't manage it. I can try to undo the damage."

"That would be amazing." Clarissa glanced at the door, her pulse beginning to race. "Can I do anything to help?"

Mr Kephisto smiled. "Just hope for the best."

He took Mrs Crouch's hand and placed it against his heart, clasping it there with one hand. With the other he lay his palm flat against her forehead. He began a chant, so quietly that Clarissa could barely hear him. The melody of his intonation, the way the words turned in and over themselves, was soft and soothing. So much so that Clarissa could feel her anxiety melting away.

The machines, meanwhile, began to pulse and spike, bells rang and beepers sounded. Clarissa stepped backwards to the door, calmly resting her palm on the handle. The nurses would arrive soon.

On the bed, Mrs Crouch jerked. Once, twice, three times. Her back arched and her mouth dropped open. She hissed and spat angrily, then sucked air, hungry to consume all of the oxygen in the room.

Someone turned the door handle. "They're here," Clarissa quietly informed Mr Kephisto.

He nodded. "We're done." He leaned down and spoke quietly to the old woman on the bed. "Time to wake up, Mrs Crouch. I command it." He nodded at Clarissa. "Open the door."

She did as he asked, turning her back to the bed for just a moment as she unlocked the door and stood back. A pair of nurses rushed in, Theresa and a colleague.

"What's going on in here?" Theresa demanded, pulling up and regarding the bed with wide eyes.

Mrs Crouch, panting as though she'd been running a marathon in her long sleep, had opened her eyes. "Yes," she gasped, craving more air. "What is going on?" She blinked in surprise at Mr Kephisto. "Who are you?"

Clarissa quickly stepped around the nurses and took Mrs Crouch's other hand. "Mrs Crouch? It's me, Clarissa. It's so good to have you back with us," she said, tears welling up in her eyes. "We've been really worried about you."

"What happened?" An expression of genuine bewilderment crossed the neighbour's pale face.

"You were at home—" Clarissa started to explain, but the confusion on Mrs Crouch's face had been quickly replaced by a frown and a widening of her eyes.

"That's right. Oh my. *That* woman. She came to my house. I saw her off."

"We need to check Mrs Crouch over," the first nurse announced rather officiously.

"Just give us two minutes," begged Clarissa. She turned back to the woman on the bed. "You saw her off?"

Mrs Crouch squeezed Clarissa's hand. "She broke into my house. Did she take anything?"

Clarissa gave a quick headshake and flashed her

eyes, hoping Mrs Crouch would take the hint not to say any more. "Nothing important."

Mrs Crouch tried to sit up, seemingly agitated. "Everything is alright," Mr Kephisto soothed her.

"You don't understand—"

"Yes, we do. *Nothing* was taken," Clarissa reassured her once more.

Mrs Crouch swallowed and settled back against the pillows. "If you're sure?"

Theresa barged past Clarissa. "I really must ask you to leave now."

"We *are* sure," Clarissa peered around the nurse's back. "But we do need your help."

Mrs Crouch glanced from Clarissa to the nurses. "Let's see about getting out of here then, shall we?"

The second nurse squawked in shock. "Mrs Crouch! I really don't think so."

"Well I do." Mrs Crouch pushed herself up into a sitting position and scowled at both nurses. "I've been a sleeper for too long." She pushed Theresa's hands away as the nurse tried to take her pulse.

"Clarissa?" She widened her eyes. "I'm quite famished. You need to give Corker's Pies a call for me, my dear."

Corker's Pies? "But—"

"You'll find the number written down on a square of paper in the footwell of your car."

Of course! Mr Kephisto had been right. Mrs Crouch had admitted it herself. She was a sleeper, and presumably a Ministry of Witches secret agent. Were Corker's Pies her handlers?

"What's the message?" Clarissa asked.

CHAPTER FIFTEEN

She left Mrs Crouch in Mr Kephisto's safe hands and returned home.

As expected, Toby had been practising his magick. Numerous cracked mugs littered the kitchen floor and, judging by the size of the accompanying puddle and the spatter pattern, he'd been trying to levitate his water bowl too.

"Good news," she told her furry friend when he rushed to the door to greet her.

"Mrs Crouch is getting well?" he asked, wagging his tail in that familiar boisterous way he had.

"Not only that, but she'll be home later today."

"Most excellent!" Toby smiled at the thought of Mrs Crouch's cheesy treats.

"I'm going to go and make sure her house is ready for her, make her bed up, maybe get some food in."

"We'll look after her," agreed Toby, happy to be of assistance.

"I just need to make a phone call." Clarissa plucked the ripped square of paper Catesby had given her weeks before. As Mrs Crouch had said, it had been in the footwell of her car, hiding beneath the rubber mat.

She keyed the number into her phone and held it to her ear. She'd forgotten all about that old-fashioned ringing noise it made.

Burr burr. Burr burr. Burr burr.

On and on it went, until she'd almost reached the stage of giving up. But Clarissa knew better now. That's what they wanted. To throw you off the scent if it wasn't important.

Finally, a clink-clunk sound, like someone physically picking up the receiver. A brief pause before a voice announced, "Corker's Pies."

A young man's voice. A clipped, polite tone. Clarissa couldn't be sure whether it was the same man she'd spoken to on the previous occasion, but it might well have been.

Clarissa hesitated fractionally, but Mrs Crouch had been adamant about the message. She cleared her throat. "Dark forebodings," she said.

A pause on the other end. "Ma'am? Can you repeat?"

"Dark forebodings."

Clarissa knew the drill. She waited. A second later she heard someone begin to frantically type on a keyboard.

"Thank you, Ma'am."

More typing. "Ah, Ma'am?"

"Yes?"

"Ma'am, on this occasion I have a return message for you."

"Shall I get a pen?" Clarissa scrabbled among the clutter on her desk. Plenty of paper, a blunt pencil, but never a biro when you needed one.

"Ma'am, we would prefer that you never ever write things down," the voice told her, still professional, still friendly enough, but with an edge of steel.

"Of course." What had she been thinking? "What's the message?"

The voice recited slowly, "I'll see you on the bark side of the moon."

"The *bark* side of the moon?"

"Yes, Ma'am."

"Who is the message from? Who will I meet there?"

"I'm afraid I don't have that information, Ma'am. That is all. Thank you for calling—"

"Wait—"

"That is all," the voice repeated, in total control. "Thank you for calling Corker's Pies."

The line went dead.

Clarissa stared at the screen of her phone for a moment. It turned black. She squeezed the sides until it lit up once more. On a hunch she went into her call history. The number had been removed, leaving no trace that she had spoken to anyone in the previous five minutes.

Toby nudged her. "There's a taxi outside. I think it must be Mrs Crouch."

"Already?" Clarissa jumped to her feet. "That was fast work."

"Let's go and meet her!" Toby jumped around, full of beans and enthusiasm and an unquenchable desire for cheesy treats.

"Alright, alright." With one last frown at her phone, Clarissa went to the front door. As she unlatched it, Toby gazed up at her.

"That was Old Joe's favourite piece of music, you know?"

"What was?" Clarissa asked.

"*Dark Side of the Moon.* He used to play it on the piano."

Clarissa pulled the door open and Toby flew out, barking an ecstatic welcome at a smiling, although peaky-looking, Mrs Crouch.

Clarissa glanced back at the piano, wedged tightly under the stairs. She walked back to it and lifted the lid. The music for *Dark Side of the Moon* remained on the music rack, where it had been since the last time Old Joe had tickled the ivories.

Such a strange coincidence.

Clarissa whistled long and low, the sound echoing around the empty hallway. A shiver ran down her back.

What did all this mean?

Would Old Joe meet her on the Bark Side of the Moon? Or was this some sort of complicated trap set up by Miranda Dervish?

She shuddered, recalling his last words written to her in his letter:

There is much your brothers, sisters and elders can teach you, but an important part of being a witch is listening to your instincts, particularly when instinct is the only tool you have left in your armoury.

<u>Choose your friends wisely</u>, and trust only those deserving of that gift.

Clarissa walked slowly back to the front door and watched as Mr Kephisto helped Mrs Crouch along the path. They waved at her, and Mr Kephisto mimed the turning of the key. She had it, of course, Mrs Crouch's key.

Choose her friends wisely?

As she drifted ever deeper into this mystery, she could only hope against hope that she'd made a good start on that part of his advice.

Only time would tell.

HAVE YOU ENJOYED SPELLBOUND HOUND BOOK TWO?

Have you enjoyed Spellbound Hound Book Two?

You'll find Book Three, *Bark Side of the Moon* right HERE

If you enjoyed *A Curse, a Coven and a Canine* and you'd like to see more *Spellbound Hound*, please leave me a review on Amazon or Goodreads.

Reviews help spread the word about my work, which is great for me because I find new readers!

It's also a win win for my dogs because they get a healthy dog treat for every review that's left (but no sammiches, Betsy needs to watch her weight and Finley can't cope with wheat).

And why not join my mailing list to find out more about what I'm up to and what is coming out next?

HAVE YOU ENJOYED SPELLBOUND HOUND BOOK TWO?

If you'd like to join my closed author group you'll find it here at

www.facebook.com/groups/JeannieWycherleysFiends just let me know you've reviewed one of my books when apply.

BARK SIDE OF THE MOON
SPELLBOUND HOUND BOOK 3

Bark Side of the Moon: Spellbound Hound Magic and Mystery Book 3

The Pointy Woman gave him a voice. Now she wants to shut him up.

Permanently.

Would-be investigative journalist, Clarissa Page, and her sammich-obsessed spellbound hound, Toby, are making little headway in their hunt for the nasty witch, Miranda Dervish. And they're having no luck finding the magickal Four Stone either.

No matter which way they turn, who they ask, or where they search, they're thwarted.

Down to their last few pence, an anonymous tip off and a chance encounter with a stranger in the park sets them on their way to a dramatic final showdown. On the way, they'll have to work out just who is friend… and who is foe.

Bark Side of the Moon is Book 3 of 3 of the Spellbound Hound Magic and Mystery Series. From the bestselling author of the Wonky Inn books, you'll find this cozy animal mystery is chock full of the quirky characters you've come to love. Cute pups, cunning witches, wily wizards, chaos and squizzels abound in this heart-warming 'tail' of love and loyalty.

Find it here.

READ THE WONKY INN BOOKS

The Wonkiest Witch: Wonky Inn Book 1

Alfhild Daemonne has inherited an inn.

And a dead body.

Estranged from her witch mother, and having committed to little in her thirty years, Alf surprises herself when she decides to start a new life.

She heads deep into the English countryside intent on making a success of the once popular inn. However, discovering the murder throws her a curve ball. Especially when she suspects dark magick.

Additionally, a less than warm welcome from several

locals, persuades her that a variety of folk – of both the mortal and magickal persuasions – have it in for her.

The dilapidated inn presents a huge challenge for Alf. Uncertain who to trust, she considers calling time on the venture.

Should she pack her bags and head back to London?

Don't be daft.

Alf's magickal powers may be as wonky as the inn, but she's dead set on finding the murderer.

Once a witch always a witch, and this one is fighting back.
A clean and cozy witch mystery.

Take the opportunity to immerse yourself in this fantastic new witch mystery series, from the author of the award-winning novel, *Crone*.

Grab Book 1 of the Wonky Inn series, *The Wonkiest Witch,* on Amazon now.

THE WONKY INN SERIES

The Wonkiest Witch: Wonky Inn Book 1
The Ghosts of Wonky Inn: Wonky Inn Book 2
Weird Wedding at Wonky Inn: Wonky Inn Book 3
The Witch Who Killed Christmas: Wonky Inn Christmas Special
Fearful Fortunes and Terrible Tarot: Wonky Inn Book 4
The Mystery of the Marsh Malaise: Wonky Inn Book 5
The Mysterious Mr Wylie: Wonky Inn Book 6
The Great Witchy Cake Off: Wonky Inn Book 7
Vengeful Vampire at Wonky Inn: Wonky Inn Book 8
Witching in a Winter Wonkyland: A Wonky Inn Christmas Cozy Special

ALSO BY

Midnight Garden: The Extra Ordinary World Novella Series Book 1 (2019)

Beyond the Veil

Crone

A Concerto for the Dead and Dying

(short story, 2018)

Deadly Encounters: A collection of short stories

Keepers of the Flame: A love story

Non-Fiction

Losing my best Friend

Thoughtful support for those affected by dog bereavement or pet loss

Follow Jeannie Wycherley

Find out more at on the website

www.jeanniewycherley.co.uk

You can tweet Jeannie

twitter.com/Thecushionlady

Or visit her on Facebook for her fiction

www.facebook.com/jeanniewycherley

Sign up for Jeannie's newsletter

eepurl.com/cN3Q6L

COMING IN 2020

The Municipality of Lost Souls by Jeannie Wycherley

Described as a cross between Daphne Du Maurier's *Jamaica Inn*, and TV's *The Walking Dead*, but with ghosts instead of zombies, *The Municipality of Lost Souls* tells the story of Amelia Fliss and her cousin Agatha Wick.

In the otherwise quiet municipality of Durscombe, the inhabitants of the small seaside town harbour a deadly secret.

Amelia Fliss, wife of a wealthy merchant, is the lone voice who speaks out against the deadly practice of the wrecking and plundering of ships on the rocks in Lyme bay, but no-one appears to be listening to her.

COMING IN 2020

As evil and malcontent spread like cholera throughout the community, and the locals point fingers and vow to take vengeance against outsiders, the dead take it upon themselves to end a barbaric tradition the living seem to lack the will to stop.

Set in Devon in the UK during the 1860s, *The Municipality of Lost Souls* is a Victorian Gothic ghost story, with characters who will leave their mark on you forever.

If you have previously enjoyed *Crone* or *Beyond the Veil*, you really don't want to miss this novel.

Sign up for my newsletter or join my Facebook group today.

MORE DARK FANTASY FROM JEANNIE WYCHERLEY

Crone

A twisted tale of murder, magic and salvation.

Heather Keynes' teenage son died in a tragic car accident.
Or so she thinks.

However, deep in the countryside, an ancient evil has awoken ... intent on hunting local residents.
No-one is safe.

When Heather takes a closer look at a series of coincidental deaths, she is drawn reluctantly into the company of an odd group of elderly Guardians. Who are they, and what is their connection to the Great Oak?

Why do they believe only Heather can put an end to centuries of horror?

Most important of all, who is the mysterious old woman in the forest and what is it that feeds her anger?

When Heather determines the true cause of her son's death, she is hell-bent on vengeance. Determined to halt the march of the Crone once and for all, hatred becomes Heather's ultimate weapon and furies collide to devastating effect.

Crone – winner of a *Chill with a Book Readers' Award* (February 2018) and an *Indie B.R.A.G Medallion* (November 2017).

Praise for *Crone*

'A real page turner, hard to put down.'
'Stunningly atmospheric! Gothic & timeless set in the beautifully described Devon landscape …. Twists and turns, nothing predictable or disappointing.' – Amazon reviewer

MORE DARK FANTASY FROM JEANNIE WYCHERLEY

'Atmospheric, enthralling story-telling, and engaging characters' – Amazon Reviewer

'Full of creepy, witchy goodness' – The Grim Reader

'Wycherley has a talent for storytelling and a penchant for the macabre' – Jaci Miller

Beyond the Veil

Adam was desperate...

...and he hated himself for what he was about to do. Would it be worth it?

Being a detective wasn't always easy, but he loved the life. Investigating the murder of his ex-wife, though, made this case unusual. They may not have parted on the best of terms, but the killer needed to be found. Now Adam has a suspect with the worst alibi he's *ever* heard.

And with no fresh leads and nowhere else to turn, he finds himself having to ask a self-proclaimed witch for help.

MORE DARK FANTASY FROM JEANNIE WYCHERLEY

Can she really talk to the dead?

He doubts it.

Yet as his reality starts to unravel, chills run down his back.
Is he being watched? He needs to shake the feeling off. Not let her nonsense play with his head!

Upset the dead at your own peril...
...the nightmare is about to begin.

You'll love this occult horror, because who doesn't enjoy a good scare?

Find it now.

Warning: Do NOT read at night, alone, with no one around to watch your back.

Praise for Beyond the Veil

'A 5-star winner from Queen of the Night Terrors' – Amazon reviewer.

'Really got my heart pounding' – Amazon reviewer.

MORE DARK FANTASY FROM JEANNIE WYCHERLEY

'A nerve racking, nail-biting, spine tingling, sweat producing, thrilling storyline that keeps you on a razor's edge the entire tale' – ARC reviewer.

'Female Stephen King!' – Amazon reviewer.

Printed in Great Britain
by Amazon